# KLAYTON'S TREASURE

THEA

TEXT UCP TO 22828 TO SUBSCRIBE TO OUR MAILING LIST
If you would like to join our team, submit the first 3-4 chapters
of your completed manuscript to
Submissions@UrbanChapterspublications.com

# 1

## KLAYTON JACKSON

**Three years after Coke Gurls three ended…**

"Klayton, your order is ready at the bar!" the barista yelled.

"Danielle, get your black ass over here now," I ordered. My daughter, Danielle Jackson, was the apple of my eye, and I was blessed with her birth. She was every bit of my child as she showed signs of having batshit crazy tendencies, and I knew I was going to have a hard time with her. That was my baby girl though and no one could ever tell me any different.

"Daddy, my hot chocolate ready. I'm thirsty," Danielle whined and walked right back to my side. I grabbed her hand and grabbed our drinks from the barista with my other hand. I was at Starbucks getting us something to drink on the way home from daycare. I never knew being a single parent was so hard, until I became a father. I tipped my hat to all of these hoes— I mean women out there living their best lives, raising their kids on their own. My baby's mother died not long after giving birth to Danielle, thanks to my psychotic Norman Bates ex-girlfriend, Shae, killing her in the hospital. I ended up suing the hospital for negligence and won a settlement that I had put in a trust for Danielle for when she turned twenty-one. I always wanted to be sure my daughter would never lack for anything, even when I was dead and gone. I had been running the family business for three years now, and I could retire tomorrow because I was set for life. My grandkids' kids would have money and never have to lift a finger a day in their lives. I wanted to keep this legacy alive for the day I had a son to run it because I knew I would end up married and having more kids one day. There was also another part of me that didn't want to retire from the streets because it was all that I knew. The power that is associated with my name is something that continues to give me an adrenaline rush and I loved that niggas feared me.

I turned to walk out of the door with my daughter and the cup holder holding my drinks when a female ran smack dab into my chest, causing the drinks to fall to the ground.

"Watch where the fuck your ass is going, looking like a fucking Eskimo that escaped from the fucking zoo!" I yelled.

"Fuck fuck fuck!" Danielle chanted as she jumped up and down.

"Nigga, you didn't have to be so fucking rude. Now you got your child cussing—" The woman fussed, and I finally got a closer look at her and realized it was Treasure Glover, the girl I wanted to pursue three years ago, but the timing was off at the time.

"Treasure, is that you? How the hell did you miss a big ass nigga like me?" I calmed down, seeing the most beautiful woman I had ever laid eyes on. She was a little thicker than I remembered from the last time I saw her, but she still had that long silky black hair that I wanted to run my hands through, and those kissable lips of hers had me licking my lips. She still had just enough curves to keep a nigga like me happy without it being overkill. You know those big booty hoes in those old nineties MTV music videos paid to have that shit done because there was no way that shit was real. Treasure has a nice round booty but just big enough for a nigga like me to grip and it wasn't too little.

"K-Klayton Jackson, is that you? This must be your daughter. What is your name, sweetie? My name is Treasure." She smiled at Danielle.

"Excuse me, would you guys mind not blocking the door so other customers can get in here? Please, and thank you," an older, heavyset Caucasian lady barked.

"Listen, Shamu the Whale, I didn't know they let the freaks out the fucking zoo. We will move when we are ready to fucking move—"

"Fuck you, lady!" Danielle yelled.

I grabbed my daughter and popped her on the hand, but deep down, I was cheesing like a real nigga. My daughter was bad as fuck, and I wanted her to not stand for anything with these little niggas out in the street. Truth be told, I never wanted my daughter to get married. I would provide her ass with everything that she would ever need because there wasn't going to be a nigga out here breaking her heart.

"Go sit your ass down in the chair right there."

I pointed to a table, and Danielle knew I wasn't playing with her ass. She went to do what she was told, and Treasure looked shocked at my child's mouth.

"You niggers should feel ashamed of yourselves, letting a baby talk like that—"

Before the lady could even finish her sentence, I choked her ass up and threw her against the table that held different coffee creamers and shit. Liquid and trash spilled on her, and other people looked at her in disgust for using a racial slur toward me. None of them even wanted to defend her, which was good because I had no problem laying their asses out if they tried fucking with me.

"Bitch, don't worry about how I raise my child. Worry about why you built like a mothafucking linebacker in the NFL, smelling like Old Spice. Danielle and Treasure, let's bounce before they call twelve on us."

I went to pick my daughter up, and Treasure followed us out of Starbucks.

"Klayton, did you really—"

"Treasure, don't ask something you don't want the answer to. I had screws loose before, and that still hasn't changed about me. And my dick is still long as fuck." I buckled Danielle in her car seat and turned to see Treasure blushing. I knew she was feeling a real nigga three years ago and I was attracted to her as well, but the timing was bad. Maybe it was fate that I ran into Treasure three years later and reconnected. I wasn't going to let this opportunity slip away from me this time.

"Yeah, that lady did ask for that shit, with her racist comments, but we need to get out of here before the police get here. Take my number, Klayton, and maybe we can reconnect sometime," Treasure whispered as she handed me her iPhone. I dialed my number and called myself from her phone so I had her number. There was something about Treasure that drew me to her naturally. She has a positive spirit and I found myself wanting to be around her without even trying to have sex with her.

"I definitely will be calling you so we can link up sometime, Treasure. Make sure you text me when you get home so I know you that you are safe." I felt butterflies in the pit of my stomach when looking at Treasure. Something told me that our season was on its way, no matter how much I fought my attraction toward her.

# TREASURE GLOVER

I pulled up to the house I shared with my brother, Luca, deep in thought. I never thought I would see Klayton again after everything went down three years ago, and that nigga was aging like fine wine. My first thought when I saw him was how many times I would cum if I sat on his face, especially after he went off on me the way he did for wasting his drinks. I smiled as I noticed he saved his number in my phone as Zaddy and future bae. Well, let me get you guys up to date with what is going on with me now. I graduated with my bachelor's degree last year in psychology and was in my first year specializing in counseling at USC. I still struggled with schizophrenia and PTSD from the things I went through in the past, but I learned to embrace it and it has made me stronger. I have been taking my medication faithfully and have been able to take lower amounts which has been wonderful. My daughter, Genesis, is about to turn four years old soon, and she is truly a blessing in my life. I am so grateful to my parents, Giovanni and Hope Glover, for stepping up to the plate and raising my daughter so I could focus on my education. I vowed to regain full custody of her as soon as I finished school and was settled with a house of my own I was finally in a place where it didn't hurt me to look at my daughter or interact with her and that came from a ton of therapy and working on myself. I was ecstatic when my parents finally got married a year and a half ago and finally got their happily ever after. My brother, Luca, has been depressed ever since AJ died three years ago and has been overworking himself. Part of the reason I moved in with my brother was to make sure he had a hot meal to come home to and someone to keep him company. I refused to lose my brother because of a broken heart. He called himself his sister's keeper, but in reality, it was my turn to be my brother's keeper, and I refused to let him down. Luca still has his own demons that he is battling and he never got over the past so I needed to be there for him.

"Luca, are you home?" I called out as I walked inside the home with my backpack. I placed it on the couch and went into the kitchen, where I saw Luca reading paperwork at the kitchen table.

"Hey, sis, I didn't hear you. How was class?" Luca asked. He got up and gave me a hug.

"It was good. I have a test on family systems theories coming up, so I am going to be studying for that after I call and check on Genesis and cook our dinner. Have you eaten today?" I knew I was nagging, but I had to make sure Luca was good. After AJ died, he let himself go for a period of time and was really just now starting to get back to himself. There was no time limit on grief, and I knew Luca really loved AJ. The problem was, AJ was incapable of loving my brother the way that he deserved to be loved.

"I am fine, sis. I had some pasta earlier." Luca tried to wave me off, but I knew he was lying.

"Luca, look at me, please. I know you are still grieving, but I know you are a broken man. Let me take care of you and make sure you are good." I wrapped my arms around Luca and held my brother in my arms. The thing is, Luca, prided himself on being the man of the house since our father wasn't in our lives at the time. He had too much responsibility from an early age and it made him into the workaholic that he is now.

"Sis, I am supposed to take care of you, and not vice versa. Every time I look at you, I feel like I failed you, and I miss AJ. I don't think I will ever love another woman the way I loved AJ. I feel like I am merely existing and not living life anymore," Luca admitted. My heart broke for my brother because he had to be the strong one for years, and he was finally starting to crack a bit. I would do anything to make sure he was good.

"Bro, look at me. Everything that happened to me happened for a reason, and I promise you I survived it and it made me the woman I am today. I wouldn't have Genesis if everything didn't play out the way it did. I really want you to get some individual counseling. I am worried about you." I sat in Luca's lap.

After everything went down, my parents, Luca, and I did family counseling together, and it helped us get closer as a family. The problem was, Luca needed individual counseling to work through AJ's death and the guilt he still lived with, and he refused to go because he claimed he didn't need the help. He said he was good when, in reality, my brother was a mere shell of himself.

"Treasure, I promise you, I am good. Man, my firm is thriving and my clientele is growing. You have grown so much, and I am proud of you. You are going to be an amazing counselor, and I can't wait to see what the future has in store for you." Luca finally had a genuine smile on his face. I never thought that my brother and I would be close again after everything that we went through and I would die for my brother.

"Thank you, big bro. I love you, and I am glad we are close again like we used to be. I got some steaks defrosting and I was thinking maybe a salad and baked potatoes to go with it. How does that sound?" I asked Luca.

"Let me get the grill going, sis, since you insist on making sure I eat. Go ahead and get some studying done, and I got dinner. I can't wait to see you graduate, Treasure. Stay focused and don't start fucking with these niggas in the streets, sis," Luca warned me and got up to start seasoning the steaks.

"Luca, you know I am focused on my degree and spending time with Genesis. I don't have time to date anyone, nor do I want to," I lied as my mind started wandering to thoughts of Klayton again...

# LUCA GLOVER

I was glad that my sister moved back in with me after everything happened in *Coke Gurls part three* so I could keep a better eye on her and protect her better. Treasure made me so proud of her. She finished her bachelor's at an accelerated pace in about two years, and I could see the growth in her. Part of me worried that she would throw it away behind some ain't shit street nigga, but my sister truly appeared to be on the right track.

My phone rang, and I saw it was my parents calling me.

"Hello?" I answered the phone.

"Hey son, how are you doing? How is Treasure doing?" Pops asked. It was weird to finally call him Pops, but that showed the growth in our relationship. Three years ago I hated the ground that my father walked on.

"She is doing good, man. Been busy applying herself in school. I am so proud of her," I admitted.

"Your mom and I want to bring Genesis to come to see you guys soon, if you guys have room for us—"

"You already know there is room at the house for you, Pops. Don't even say such stupid shit. I got a room for you and Mom and a room equipped for Genesis. I can't wait to see my niece, and I know Treasure would want to see her," I admitted.

"Is Treasure anywhere near you? I wanted to tell you something, but I don't want you to tell Treasure yet," my dad whispered. That made me feel kind of uncomfortable because the last thing I needed was to keep anything away from my sister, especially now that our bond was solid again.

"Man, I really don't want to keep secrets—"

"I get that, but I don't want Treasure worrying about Genesis. I need her to stay focused on completing her degree and if I tell her this now, then she will be distracted," my father explained.

"What is it, Dad?" I could tell he needed to vent. Our relationship had improved, but we still had awkward moments.

"I found a doctor in LA that does corneal transplants, and there is a possibility that Genesis might regain her vision. I don't want to tell Treasure until we are certain that this surgery will happen for Genesis. When we come to visit you guys, I have an appointment with Dr. Henry Schulman, a renowned ophthalmologist. He wants to see Genesis and see if she is a qualified candidate for the surgery," my father explained, and I was shocked.

This was an amazing opportunity available for my niece, and I prayed this would come through. "You got my word I won't say anything, Pops. This would only stress Treasure out and until we know for certain, there is no need to say anything," I agreed with my dad. Ultimately, we were looking out for Treasure and wanted the best for her.

"Thank you, son. I apologize if I am putting you in an awkward position, but I wanted to give you the heads up. I am going to email you our flight information. You don't have to pick us up from LAX as I plan to rent a car—"

"Dad, I will pick you guys up. I can do a half day at the office, if need be. You know I have plenty of cars you guys can drive. How long do you plan to keep this from Treasure?" I asked.

"Just until we know whether Genesis qualifies for the eye

surgery. I don't want to get her hopes up for nothing," my father explained. I understood exactly where he was coming from because I didn't want my sister to get her hopes up for nothing.

"Cool, that works for me."

"How are you really doing, son? I can tell you have been depressed lately. I really think you should see a counselor. Your mother and I are worried about you," my father admitted, and he sounded like a carbon copy of Treasure.

I don't know why everyone kept insisting I was depressed. I knew that I wasn't the same person since the love of my life had died, but if you asked me, I learned to adapt to life without AJ. I was doing just fine, focusing on family and my growing law firm, and no one could tell me any different.

"Dad, you sound like Treasure. I am fine although with the holidays coming up, I know it will be tough. I will always love AJ, but I have you guys and my law firm. I will be fine like, I always am."

Truth be told, I was trying to convince myself that I was good when, in reality, that was the furthest thing from the truth. Losing the love of your life takes a toll on you and it hasn't gotten any easier three years later.

"Luca, I love you. I wish you would let us be there for you instead of pushing us away. I know that you loved AJ, but she wouldn't want this for you. She would want you to live her life and honor her memory. It is okay to move on with your life and live life. You aren't fully living, son." My father was right. Part of me wanted to change that, but I had no idea how to go about doing that.

"I am fine. If I get worse, I promise I will make an appointment to see a counselor." I said that just to shut my father up because I had no intention of going to see a counselor. There was nothing wrong with me. It was normal for a man to grieve the loss of the woman he fell in love with. So what if it had been three years? There was no time limit on grief.

"That is all I can ask of you, son. Let me let you go and check on your mother as she was putting Genesis to bed. I will give your niece a kiss for you. Get some rest, son."

"Tell Mom I love her," I said and hung up the phone.

Honestly, I was truly blessed. They say that life is funny and when a life is taken, one is given to you. Before AJ had died, we found out my mother was still alive, which was a minor miracle after being shot in the head and being left for dead in a house fire. I knew that I needed to count my own blessings some more, but what I really needed was a sign from AJ telling me that it was okay to move on with my life.

# KLAYTON

"What are you thinking about, bro?" Rolonda asked me, and she had startled me. I didn't even hear Ro walk into the room. Trayce and his family came over, and little Matthew was busy playing with his cousin, Danielle, in her room. Trayce was outside lighting up the grill, and my mouth watered at the thought of some ribs and potato salad. Let me tell you, Rolonda's potato salad was official, unlike those hoes out there buying the Kroger brand of potato salad and disguising it as their own. One bitch decided to put raisins in her potato salad. Who the fuck does that?

"Man, you won't believe who I ran into recently, sis. I have been fighting my feelings for Treasure for three years, and it was fate I ran into her ass at Starbucks. I knew Luca wouldn't approve, so I didn't even try Treasure when I met her, but I can't get her out of my mind."

Ro looked at me sympathetically. "Who would have ever thought that Klayton mothafucking Jackson would have grown up? Seriously though, it isn't a good idea because of your history with Luca. You guys already don't get along because you fucked AJ, and he would see you dating Treasure as a major violation.

Treasure also doesn't deserve to be hurt if you are only pursuing her because she is the forbidden fruit."

"I know, but I can't help but want to get to know her on some real shit. I am not even on that type of time of trying to fuck hoes anymore. I can tell Treasure has been through so much, and I want to help her heal from the pain. She carries herself differently than these broads in the streets, and she can handle my crazy. I never thought I would ever have serious feelings for another woman after Shae, but Treasure is everything," I admitted. There was something about her and I just had to have her. It was deeper than lust and I wanted to make love to Treasure's mind.

"You deserve to be happy, Klayton. Be sure that Treasure is what you really want, though, for both of your sakes. She has been through more than a woman twice her age has, and it is up to her to share her story with you. You also deserve to be happy, and I am glad you finally let the guilt of AJ's death go. We all know what happened wasn't your fault." Ro comforted me. I appreciated it because some days, I still wondered *what if I handled things with Shae differently?*

"Thanks, sis. AJ didn't deserve to die behind her bullshit. I still feel like Luca hates me and I know we will never be friends, but if I do decide to pursue Treasure, we will have to be around each other. There is a lot I have to think about with pursuing, Treasure but she is worth it, sis."

"If Treasure means that much to you, then you have my blessing. Just know that true love isn't easy and you guys will go through things together, but it will be worth it. If you truly care about Treasure, then don't give up on her. You also can't treat her like one of those sluts you give community dick to," Ro warned. I knew that everything she was saying was true. I didn't blame Ro for having doubts because of my past history with women.

"I wouldn't even pursue Treasure if I was just looking to bust a nut. I can see my future with Treasure, and everything I have been through has prepared me to be the nigga she needs in her life. When she does get this pipe, I make her crazy behind this shit," I bragged as I grabbed my package.

"Nigga, you are nasty as fuck. Let me go check on the kids," Ro fussed as she left the room. I grabbed a couple of Budweisers from the refrigerator that I kept locked. Danielle was bad as fuck, and I had to lock shit up to keep her from getting into it. I made sure to keep alcohol in a separate refrigerator than the one I kept the food in.

I walked outside to see Trayce manning the grill, and I handed him a beer. "Good looking, nigga. Now, what is on your mind?"

I was so grateful for the fact that Trayce forgave me for sleeping with his ex-wife before they got married. When I was in the reckless stage of my life in my early twenties, I fucked Charlotte and didn't even tell him and let him marry the broad. It eventually came out and it took a lot of work, but my brother eventually forgave me. I started thinking with my big head instead of my little head (wait, ain't shit little about Klayton fucking Jackson) and have grown up a lot. I still make mistakes, but I have been a completely different man and am proud of my growth.

"Man, I was just talking to Ro and I told her I ran into Treasure Glover the other day—"

"Man, did you lose whatever fucking marbles you got in your mind? I know exactly where you are going with this and hell naw! You have already let enough bitches sample your dick in LA, and Treasure is not one you should play with," Trayce warned as he flipped the ribs on the grill.

"Come on, man, give me some credit. You know I am not out there fucking bitches anymore, man. All I have is that one dip, and I don't even fuck her like that now." I was frustrated because I needed my brother's support. I needed him to believe in me and see that I had changed, and I wasn't sure how to make him see it. I did have a dip that I had been fucking on and off for the last year, but it was nothing serious and we both knew what time it was. I told Jennifer from jump street it was nothing but sex, and only when I called her between booty call hours. I didn't care to hear about her sob stories or situations with her baby fathers or what was going on in our lives. When I came through, it was to bust a nut and that was it, and honestly, I don't even fuck with Jennifer very often. I usually fucked her once a month, just to keep her from getting attached to the dick. I had enough of these crazy bitches to last a lifetime.

"If you are serious about pursuing Treasure, then you need to come at her correct, Klayton. You know it is all love over here, bruh, but it will start a fucking war if you break her heart. You know Luca never truly forgave you for AJ's death as it is, man. You know he won't take it well when he finds out you are dating Treasure." Trayce put the rest of the cooked meat in the tray, and I grabbed it out of his hands. I placed it on the table and wrapped it with aluminum foil.

"No disrespect, but I am my own man and I fear no nigga. Luca bleeds like I do, and Treasure is a grown ass woman. If she chooses to date me, then that is her choice and if I have to go to blows with Luca, I will. Treasure needs Zaddy in her life to get her all the way together," I bragged. The thing about me was when I fell in love, I loved hard. I would protect Treasure with everything in me as long as she gave me a chance. I knew that the man I used to be wasn't ready for the love Treasure had to offer, but the man I was becoming was ready to step up and claim my future wife.

# 3

## TREASURE

"Yo Treasure, when are you going to let me take you to my house and let you ride my dick?" My classmate, Darnell, whispered in my ear just as class had ended for the day. Darnell was this little cornball nigga that thought because he was good looking and came from a wealthy family that he was entitled to pussy. What he didn't know was I was from the hood and fully with the shits. My ass took some self-defense classes, and the empowerment self-defense (ESD) courses really helped in my healing process from my trauma.

"I will ride your dick when hell freezes over, pigs fly out of the sky, and you grow a pussy. Fuck off, jackass." I shoved his ass out of the way and grabbed my phone out of my pocket. I was prepared to call my brother if need be because Luca would get up here and kill his ass on campus. It wasn't easy, but I walked briskly toward the new Mercedes Luca bought for me last year and threw my textbooks in the car. I prayed I did well on the test I just took. I had been studying hard for this exam, and all the different counseling theories was confusing for me to learn. I drove off bumping Cardi and decided to reward myself with some

Popeyes. Lord knows Thea's crazy ass loves her some Popeyes, so I love the shits too since she invented my ass.

I got home and went in my room with my food since Luca wasn't home. Lord knows I wanted to text Klayton, but I didn't want to appear to be thirsty. Instead of texting him like I wanted, I started scrolling down my Facebook page, which was set to private. After what I went through, I became a very private person and did not take to strangers easily. My phone rang and I saw Klayton was calling me, so I answered the phone.

"Hey, what's up?" I took a bite of my chicken leg.

"Hey, Treasure. It is me, Klayton. Is this a good time to talk?"

"Yeah, I am just eating some Popeyes. This shit is bussing, nigga."

"Let me have a piece. You know I'm a big man. I need a woman to come bring me and my daughter some food," Klayton clowned.

"Yo, you know Uber Eats delivers, right?" I asked. It felt good to have some back and forth banter and not feel like I was on the defensive with Klayton. For some reason, I felt a protective vibe from Klayton. I didn't know him very well, but I just felt safe with him.

"Yeah, but that isn't the same. I want to see you, Treasure. There is something about you that draws me to you, and I just want to protect you. I know Luca and I have history, but I promise you I am not on no fuck shit—"

"Klayton, I believe you. I never would have given you my number if I thought you were on some fuck boy shit. I just finished taking a test today, and I actually would like to get out of the house."

"Is it okay if I come pick you up and I can take you out on a real date? You don't have to dress up, but I would like to take you to the beach and maybe to dinner," Klayton explained.

"That sounds good, although I am full from the Popeyes now.

Maybe we can go out for coffee and talk. Besides, I kind of owe you a drink since I wasted y'alls stuff the last time." I giggled at how mad Klayton got at the time. I don't know how I didn't see that big ass nigga, but I ran right into him.

"I will pick you up tonight at seven pm. Let me let you go so I can get my brother to let Danielle stay the night with him and I will pick you up later."

**Later that evening...**

Klayton was supposed to pick me up in an hour, and I was nervous about what to wear. I had just finished taking a shower and kept changing outfits because I didn't like anything I had chosen for the date. I decided to call Brii and get some advice from her on what to wear.

"Hey sis, what's up? How is school going?" Brii asked.

"School is going well, sis. How are you and Jonah doing? I need to come see Antoinette and Blake again soon."

"Girl, they are fine and flourishing in school. They are doing really good. I was concerned about how the past would affect them when they started school, but no problems. I still have them in therapy once a week, though, because they still don't like playing with other kids very much. Now, I know you didn't call me to kee kee about your niece and nephew," Brii fussed. Technically, Antoinette and Blake and I were not blood related, but I loved them like they were. Jonah and Brii got married two years ago and I was waiting on them to have a baby, but I knew they already had a full household with Leslie, who was now five years old; Antoinette and Blake were five and seven years old. Blake was very overprotective of his sister, and Antoinette tended to cling to Blake a lot.

"So, I need your advice, sis. I have a date tonight, and I can't decide what to wear. I was going to wear this red Versace dress with a pair of Valentino pumps, but it makes my ass look too big," I complained.

"Bitch, you better tell me who you going on a date with, especially since Luca has screws loose over you. Remember that nigga Terrance that asked you out at the Labor Day barbecue and his body came up missing? This nigga must have a death wish—"

"Girl please, Luca needs to let me live my life and not stay stuck in the past. He still blames himself for what happened to me, and I know it because he refuses to let me go on a date. He thinks I should only focus on school and building a relationship with Genesis, but I deserve to be happy as well," I explained. I was tired of living in the little bubble Luca had placed me in.

"Do you want me to try to talk to him, sis? You deserve to be able to live a happy life and date, like a young woman your age typically does. He feels like he is sheltering you when, in reality, he is keeping you from moving on with your life."

"Not yet, sis. I know he is still depressed, and I am trying to convince him to go into therapy. I feel like my brother is a shell of himself. Maybe I should cancel my date—"

"Treasure, no! You need to start living life and do what makes you happy. Who is it that is risking their life to take you out?" Brii asked.

"I ran into Klayton Jackson's big ass at a Starbucks and we reconnected—"

"Lawd, please don't tell me you are going out with Klayton. Klayton and Luca might end up killing each other because they never completely squashed their beef from years ago. If you and Klayton start dating and it becomes serious, it could squash any peace they might have had. Are you prepared to deal with that?"

I didn't even think about how Luca would feel about me dating one of the Jackson brothers, especially considering the past drama. Maybe I should leave Klayton alone but there was something about that man that naturally drew me to him. I couldn't help my strong attraction towards him.

"Shit, I didn't even think about that. I just figured Luca would have a hard time dealing with the fact that I want to go out on a date."

I didn't even hear Luca walk in my room because I was too engrossed in my conversation with Brii.

"Who do you think you are going out on a date with?"

# LUCA

The second I heard Treasure talking to Brii about going on a date, I felt like I was going to lose my mind. In my eyes, Treasure was still that teenager that had been taken advantage of, and I had a second chance to protect her and make sure she was good. None of these niggas in LA meant her any good, and none of them were good enough for my sister to date, let alone marry. It was time to nip that date shit in the bud because I was not having it one bit.

"Luca, what are you doing in my room? Brii, let me call you tomorrow." Treasure hung up.

"Go get dressed, sis, and don't think about putting on that tiny ass hoe dress. If you think you are about to go out on a date, then you will be sorely disappointed when I tell you the answer is no," I warned her.

"Luca, I am not a child and you will not treat me like one. You forget that I am a grown woman and went through things women twice my age wouldn't be able to handle. I am twenty-one, and you can't shelter me from the world forever, bro."

"Why do you need to date, Treasure? You are working on your master's degree and are about to become a counselor. You are living life and have a lot to look forward to, including building a relationship with Genesis. That should be your focus and not another nigga," I reminded Treasure. Part of me felt like she should be focusing more on becoming a mother to Genesis because she did not ask to be here. If I was completely honest, I kind of resented Treasure because her daughter was being raised by our parents when that wasn't their responsibility. Granted, she was forced to have the baby when she made it known she wanted an abortion but I still felt that she could have been doing more for Genesis.

"Nigga, are you really saying I don't love my child? Why are you trying to make me feel bad for wanting to live my best life? You are a bitter man, Luca, and AJ's death changed your ass. I don't know the man you have become, and I am not liking what I am seeing. You really need to get some help." Treasure's disrespectful ass decided to come out of the bathroom wearing the dress that I specifically told her not to wear.

"I just told your ass not to put on that fucking dress. You are not going on a date, and you are not going out there looking like a whore, and that is final!" I snapped before I stomped out of the room.

I didn't even hear Jonah walk in the house, but felt him slap me on the back. "Yo Luca, come on man, you need to chill. You are being way too hard on Treasure and you know it."

"What are you doing here, nigga?" I frowned. If I had known that I was in for this kind of a night when I got off of work, then I would have stayed my ass at work and focused on one of my new cases.

"Brii heard you and Treasure talking and told me to get my ass over here, and she was right. Why are you flipping on little sis?" Jonah led me toward my man cave. We walked inside and he went to grab us a couple of beers. He opened them and handed me one before he sat down.

"Treasure has been through too much, and there isn't a nigga in these streets that is good enough for her. If I am wrong, then let me be that but she deserves much more than what these LA niggas have to offer. She needs to focus on her career goals and building with Genesis. She isn't even a mother to her child and—"

"Man, you are foul as hell throwing that shit in her face. You do know how Genesis was conceived and why it has been hard for her to raise Genesis on her own. You should be the last person judging her for how she has reacted in her situation, Luca. You know better than that, man. I am disappointed in you. How the hell do you think Treasure feels knowing you are throwing her past in her face?" Jonah asked. I didn't think that I was throwing her past in her face. I just wanted her to see that she didn't need a man in her life in order to be happy.

"Bruh, I didn't even mean it like that. Like I said, she needs to get her priorities straight. She has no business entertaining a nigga until she can afford to live on her own and raise her daughter on her own without our parents' help. If that shit is throwing stones, then it is what it is and it is how I feel." I shrugged my shoulders. I refused to apologize for speaking on how I felt, even if I was dead ass wrong. Little did I know, Treasure was standing right outside of my man cave listening to what I was saying.

Treasure walked in with tears in her eyes, and I felt bad about what I just said.

"Luca, is that how you really feel? I knew that AJ's death changed you and I have been doing everything to try to get my brother back and be there for you, but I think it is best if I move out. By the way, you got your wish and I canceled my damn date, asshole. I am going out because I don't need to be around your ass." Treasure ran out of the room before I could stop her. I got up to chase her, but Jonah quickly blocked my path.

"Nah, give little sis some time. You said some really hurtful shit to her, man. You really need to get yourself together, and Treasure is right. You have changed and it hasn't been for the better. You need to wake up before you end up losing your relationship with your little sister," Jonah warned. The only reason I didn't fight to get past Jonah was that I had a tracker on her phone so I could always see where she was at as long as her phone was on.

"Man, she is just in her feelings. She will get over it once she realizes that wasn't what I meant. I promised my pops and myself that I would never fail my sister again, and if it means she doesn't date and have a life, then that is what it is. I can't bear to see Treasure hurt the way that she was in the past, and that almost broke me. I will always make sure Treasure is good financially so she doesn't need a man to take care of her, and she damn sure doesn't need to experience sex. She has enough family to make sure she isn't lonely." It was unfair, but I never truly forgave myself for the trauma that my sister went through. I still think that if I had did things differently that Blach never would have gotten anywhere near Treasure.

"Luca, you need to see a therapist and let that hurt you are carrying go, man. AJ would not want this for you, and you are punishing Treasure for the past. She has come a long way with having a relationship with Genesis and you know it. I love you, bruh, and I promise I will be here for you more, and I apologize for being a bad friend." Jonah embraced me in a brotherly hug and I wept for a couple of minutes.

I had learned in therapy that it did not make me weak for displaying emotions, and I knew that Jonah would never judge me for it. Jonah had been there for me through the trenches, and we would give our lives for each other with no questions asked.

"Man, no worries. I know you are living the family life now with Brii and you got three kids you are raising now. I feel terrible for bothering you with my problems when I have no idea what is going on with you."

"I came to check on you, bro. Everything is good on the home front, although I want to get Brii pregnant. I know we already have three kids we are raising so I wouldn't ask her to give me a football team, but does it make me a selfish nigga to want kids of my own?" Jonah asked.

"How does Brii feel about you guys having kids?" I checked my phone to see where Treasure was at and was happy to see she was at Nikki and Kobe's house. I knew she would be safe there as Kobe wouldn't let anything happen to them.

"Brii has been telling me hell no because it feels like we already have a ready-made family. She has been talking shit about getting her tubes tied, and I almost slapped her ass into tomorrow. We got in a fight last week about it and everything isn't the same because we both keep putting off the conversation," Jonah admitted.

"I mean, sis kinda has a point. You guys already have three kids between her siblings and Leslie. None of them might be biologically yours, but you are really their father. Is it really a deal breaker if Brii doesn't change her mind? Brii is probably over-whelmed with three kids and you want to add a fourth, and all because you want a biological child?" I asked. It was easy for me to say, considering I wasn't in Jonah's situation, but I was happy to finally get out of the hot seat.

"Hell yeah, it is a deal breaker. I understood her situation with her siblings and had no problem stepping up to the plate and taking care of them, but I always wanted my own kids. I never had that conversation with Brii because what is understood doesn't need to be explained."

"How the hell can you get mad at Brii when you guys never really sat down and had kids? Hell, that is a conversation you guys should have had before you got married. Take it from me, don't live your life having any regrets because you saw how my love story with AJ ended. Fix shit with Brii before your ass ends up sitting in my shoes wondering what if..."

# 4

## BRII LYONS

Yes, you read that correctly. My name is now Brii Lyons instead of
Anderson since I married the love of my life, Jonah Lyons, two
years ago. We are a family of five with Blake being the oldest at
age seven, and Antoinette and Leslie are both five years old. Last
week, Jonah brought up the idea of us having a baby since none
of the kids were toddlers anymore, and I looked at him like he
was crazy. I naturally assumed he knew that I didn't want to have
any kids of my own because I spent my childhood having to help
raise Antoinette and Blake. The mistake that I made was that I
assumed that we were on the same page about having kids. I
never got to spend time enjoying my own childhood or finding
my own identity. It was something Jonah and I should have talked
about before we got married, but I figured he wouldn't want any
biological kids when we had three that we were raising. Leslie
turned out to not have Jonah's blood, but we both grew attached
to him and legally adopted him.

"Hey, Ro. Do you have a minute to talk?" I asked.

"Girl, I will make the time. In fact, Trayce can watch the kids.
Give me fifteen and I will be there and we can have a girl's night,"
Rolonda suggested.

"Ro, you know I have the kids, right?"

"Bih, those kids better go watch Barney the fucking dinosaur and go to bed. See, what you do is you dope these little niggas up with Nyquil and knock them out."

"Rolonda, you are starting to act like your crazy ass husband," I fussed and had to stop myself from laughing. I knew that she wasn't serious about doping them with Nyquil. Ro's crazy ass hung up on me, so I went to check on the kids. Antoinette had her own room while Blake and Leslie shared a room. It was an adjustment when we all moved in together after my engagement to Jonah. We took it slowly and took a year to plan the wedding of my dreams, and Antoinette was my flower girl. It was hard not having my sister, AJ, there for one of the biggest days of my life. I always thought we would be each other's maid of honor and sometimes, I still struggled to cope with my twin sister's death.

I walked into Antoinette's princess-themed Cinderella room and saw her asleep on her pink Cinderella-themed bed with fine Egyptian sheets. After all my siblings went through, they deserved the world, and Jonah and I made sure they got it. I placed Antoinette under the blanket; she was a wild sleeper. Half of her body was almost falling out of the bed, and the last thing I needed was my sister getting hurt.

I left and went to check on the boys and saw them pretending to be asleep.

"Blake and Leslie, get your asses in bed before I take your tablets away for a week."

"We sorry, Mama Brii." Leslie stared at me. All three of the kids called me that because they were comfortable referring to me as their mom, which I guess I was, in a sense. It touched me to know I was making a difference in these kids' lives.

I kissed them both on the cheek and put the covers on them.

"Get some sleep. You both have school tomorrow. Night night." I left and closed the door.

I walked into the kitchen and grabbed some stuff to make Ro

and I some margaritas. I started making the drinks when the doorbell rang. I went to let Ro in the house and she hugged me.

"Hey, girl. I hope you got drinks ready. I took an Uber so my ass can get loaded and take an Uber home," Ro bragged.

"You know damn well Jonah isn't going to let your ass take an Uber. You better get ready to stay the night, but Trayce's crazy ass might bring the kids and drag you out of this house." Rolonda's husband, Trayce, played no games over her ass.

"I wish that nigga would try with Klayton's daughter and our son. What's going on with you?" Ro followed me to the kitchen and helped grab us some snacks, and I finished making our drinks.

"Would you think I was crazy if I said that I didn't want to have any kids of my own?" I asked. I put our drinks on a tray and carried them to the living room. Ro followed me with a tray full of chips, popcorn, and candy on it.

"I wouldn't say you were crazy, especially considering you have to raise your younger siblings. Did you and Jonah ever discuss how you guys felt about having kids?" Ro asked.

"No, I thought he understood that we had a complete family with my siblings and Leslie. I don't want to be raising a football team, Ro. I have goals and dreams of my own that I would like to accomplish," I complained. I took a sip of my drink, then placed the glass back on the table.

"You know damn well Jonah wouldn't leave you to raise these kids by yourself, Brii. Why do you think you can't pursue your dreams and have a couple of kids with Jonah? What is really going on with you, and why are you so scared? You both are to blame for not discussing this before you got married, but are you prepared to deal with the consequences?"

"What do you mean, Ro?"

"What I mean is this could be a deal breaker for Jonah, and can you handle it if he divorces you over this? Children are a deal breaker, and I honestly think if I never had my child with Trayce, he would have divorced me," Ro spoke honestly, and it shook me to my very core.

Would Jonah really leave me over something so trivial? Once we said our vows, it was for better or worse and if he could leave me that easily, was this something I was willing to fight for? Then, if Jonah did divorce me, all of the kids would have to readjust to living in a broken home with split custody, and I didn't want that for them. I had a lot to think about, and I knew I really needed to talk to Jonah. I prayed this was something that we could work through and he could come around to see my side of things. All I knew was I was unwilling to give Jonah a biological child of his own. and he could learn to accept that or we would be headed to divorce court.

# GIOVANNI GLOVER

My family and I just landed in LA, and I was eager to see my two kids again. Part of me felt guilty about the secret we were holding from Treasure, but I rationalized it as not wanting to get her hyped up about Genesis until we knew this would be a reality. As of now, the surgery to help restore Genesis' eyesight was only a possibility because the doctor needed to determine if she was a good candidate for the surgery. Genesis was a loving four-year-old who was full of life with her mother's personality, which was a blessing. None of us wanted her having any of Blach's negative psychotic personality traits.

"Are you sure we are doing the right thing? If Treasure finds out that we lied to her—" Hope looked worried as we walked toward baggage claim. Hope stopped talking when she saw our son, Luca, waving at us with a big smile on his face.

I forgot what I was going to say to Hope, and I gripped Genesis' little hand tighter. We made our way to Luca, and it felt good when he gave a genuine father-son type of hug. I never thought we would get to the point where we treated each other like family, and thanks to a ton of family counseling, we finally started to build a bond.

"How are you doing, son?" I was genuinely concerned about Luca's wellbeing. I could tell that all was not well with him when we talked the other day. I didn't tell Hope anything because I didn't want her to worry more than she already was over our kids.

"I am good, Pops. Let me give my niece a piggyback ride. Hey mom, how are you?" Luca gave Hope a hug and she hugged him tightly.

"I am happy, son. I wish you and Treasure were as happy as your father and I, and don't tell me you are okay. A mother knows her child," Hope fussed.

Luca placed his hand on her shoulder while I started looking at the conveyor belt to grab our bags. I managed to grab our bags and wheeled them toward my family.

"Up up, Uncle Luca!" Genesis yelled with a cheesy grin on her face.

"Anything for my niece, but I got you as soon as we get home. Let me help Pops with the luggage." Luca bent down to meet Genesis at eye level. She pouted and had all of us laughing. Genesis had all of us spoiled, and there was nothing that we wouldn't do for her.

Luca led us to his car, and we made it to Luca's home in about twenty minutes. "When will Treasure get home from school?"

"She usually comes home around three pm because she prefers morning courses this semester. She should be home any minute now, and she will be happy to see you guys," Luca reassured us. We went into the house and got settled in the rooms we stayed in whenever we came to visit. Luca had a special room with Disney princesses made especially for Genesis whenever she visited. It was always hard to get her to leave because she loved it here so much.

We left Genesis to play with her wheely bug toy that was designed to help with coordination and vision. Her room was child-proofed where there was almost nothing she could bump into and get hurt. She also had a toy singalong CD player she liked playing with and singing to the music. The buttons were very easy for her to find, and she also loved her Light Stax illuminated construction blocks that lit up.

"Let me go in the kitchen and see what Luca has to cook. Thank god Treasure is here; otherwise, he would have this place looking like the typical bachelor's pad," Hope fussed and I laughed at her. Truth be told, Hope and I loved it in New York, but every time we came to visit our children, we were reminded that we left a piece of ourselves in California.

I decided to go check on Luca and I found him in his office, deep in thought. I walked in and took a seat across from him. I never thought I would see the day that Luca would be comfortable enough to confide in me and that we would become close.

"What is going on, son?"

"Man, I think I fucked up with Treasure. I got mad at her the other day because she wanted to go on a date. I tried to tell her she couldn't go and she hasn't talked to me since," Luca admitted.

I felt guilty because I knew Luca continued to blame himself for the past, and it wasn't his fault. All I wanted was for my kids to be able to live their best lives. Luca was holding Treasure back due to the guilt he carried about the past and it was unfair to both of them.

"Son, you don't have to play the father role anymore. I know I messed up a lot with the choices I made, and I can't apologize to you guys enough—"

"Pops, what happened wasn't your fault. You did what you thought was best at the time and were only trying to protect us. I can't fault you for that. I was supposed to protect my mother and my sister and I failed. No one can tell me any differently," Luca insisted, and he had tears in his eyes.

I wish I could take the pain he was feeling away from him. The worst feeling in the world was seeing your children in pain and realizing there was nothing you could do to help them.

"You never should have had the weight of the world on your

shoulders, son. Honestly, it is wrong for me to have asked you to keep what I told you the other day a secret because I am realizing that I put more of a burden on you than you deserve. You have to let Treasure live life and date because otherwise, that sick piece of shit continues to have power over you guys from the grave. I have never been more proud than I have been to see you and Treasure glow up from the shit you guys went through. You might not feel like you are stronger for it, but you are. Don't let anyone tell you differently, but a real man does feel emotions and it doesn't make you weak. I love you so much Luca and I am sorry that I placed so much responsibility on you at an early age."

Luca collapsed on the ground in tears, and I went to embrace him. I knew that he hadn't fully healed from everything that happened in the past, and I felt helpless. They say time heals all wounds, but it felt like time was only making things worse for my son.

# 5

## TREASURE

I got an A on my counseling theories exam and I was happy. All of the hard work I was putting in on my education was for Genesis because she deserved it. I vowed that one day, I would be able to give her the life that she deserved and to be fully present in her life like she deserved. Part of the reason I allowed my parents to take custody of her three years ago was because I knew I still had healing and emotional work to do on myself. When I started my master's program, one of my professors talked to us about self-care and being able to recognize our personal triggers. The longer I was in this program, the more I was learning about myself and how strong of a woman I am for all that I have endured.

"Ms. Glover, you will be doing the role play with Mr. Miller, and you will be playing the counselor. He will be the patient. Remember, the point of this is to get practice so do not feel like you have to do everything correctly." Ms. Ramirez smiled.

I tried not to roll my eyes as I got to the center of the class to see Darnell's ass cheesing at the idea of being close to me. There was something about him that makes my skin crawl and I really didn't want to be around him if I didn't have to. Unfortunately, I had this doofus in a few of my classes and most of the time, he didn't seem to apply himself during the lectures. I was eager to get this over with so I could go home and relax. I wanted to call Klayton and make up for that botched date the other night. Luca had upset me to where I wasn't even in the mindset to go on a date anymore, and I ended up spending the night at Nikki and Kobe's house.

"Hello, Mr. Miller. My name is Treasure, and I will be your counselor for today. What brings you in to see me today?" I asked with a fake smile on my face.

"My name is Darnell, and my parents are making me come in because I believe in grabbing women by the pussy. There is this one slim thick woman I have had my eyes on for a while, and she isn't giving me any play—"

My legs started shaking because he had just triggered me by mentioning a reference to rape. I also knew that he was referring to me as the woman that wasn't giving him any action. It was taking everything in me to keep my cool. I wanted to kick his ass in his genital area but I didn't want to risk getting kicked out of school.

"Darnell, why do you think it is okay to grab women by the pussy? If that woman isn't giving you any play, as you call it, then you should move on and find a woman that is interested in you."

Granted, Darnell didn't know about my personal history with sexual assault, but there was some shit you just shouldn't say, especially shit that encouraged rape culture.

"Treasure, my father always raised me to be aggressive and go after what I want, regardless of who it hurts. She might not want me, but I had my eyes on her since the first day of school with that little onion-shaped booty of hers and that long black hair that I would love to pull when I am giving backshots—"

"Mr. Miller, that is enough! I would hate to have you permanently removed from my class, but I will if you do not tread lightly. You need to leave and come back next week. I will send you your assignments via email, and this is the only warning you will get. Ms. Glover, I apologize that he made you feel uncomfortable." Ms. Ramirez apologized, but what happened wasn't her fault. Darnell wasn't even smart enough to hide who he was referring to when he referred to forcing himself on a woman. Luckily my professor caught on because I was about to mace his ass in front of the entire class.

"I am fine." I was trying to reassure myself more than I was my professor, but she wasn't even buying it.

"Give it a few minutes and if you need to leave, I am sure one of your classmates can give you the notes for the lecture I am going to do in a bit. I understand that you might not feel like finishing class for the day, and remember what I have said about self-care," Ms. Ramirez reminded me. She knew about my trauma history because I confided in her after class one day to let her know that I had certain things that were triggers for me.

"Thank you. I appreciate it." I started gathering my things to leave and waited another ten minutes before I felt like it was safe to leave. One of my classmates named Darius decided to escort me to my car, which I appreciated as it made me feel slightly less paranoid.

I made it home fifteen minutes later and sat in my car for a few minutes to get myself together. I was pleasantly surprised to walk inside and smell food cooking in the kitchen, and I heard my mom singing.

"Mommy!" I yelled and I walked into the kitchen. The sight of my mother made my day much better than it had been going.

"Treasure! I missed you!" My mom put the spoon down from stirring the collard greens she was cooking and wrapped me in her arms tightly. We hugged for a couple of minutes before I reluctantly let go.

"How is Genesis doing? I need to go check on my baby girl." I left and walked past Luca's office, where I saw my brother and father having a serious conversation. I walked inside Genesis' room and saw her playing with one of her toys.

"Hey Genesis, how are you?" I walked up to her and held her in my arms. It seemed like it was just yesterday when Genesis was born, and now she had gotten so big.

"Hi, Treasure. How are you?" Genesis signed to me in sign language. Her speech was delayed for her age, and my parents had her working with a speech therapist to learn to talk. Another thing was I agreed with my parents that she should call them mom and dad and when she was old enough to understand, I would introduce myself as her mother. I got to be the cool big sister that spent time with her and developed a relationship with her, without the responsibility. Part of me felt guilty because I knew I should have a bigger role in her life and should be raising her. I wanted to get myself in a financial position where my daughter would want for nothing.Right now she was better off with my parents but I could not wait for the day that I would have sole physical custody of my daughter. I also wanted to explain to her while she was young that I am really her mother but that was a conversation that I needed to sit down with my parents and have.

"Can I play with you?" I asked her. I had been getting better with my sign language so I would be able to communicate her in the event she ever regained her vision. Part of me still held out hope that there was some sort of miracle that would help her regain her vision. I wanted Treasure to be able to go to school and live a full life like other children, and I was worried about her being bullied because she was blind. When Genesis was younger, my parents taught her sign language so she would have a form of communication since she has always struggled with her speech.

Genesis signed 'yes' to me, and I settled in to play with my child. As much as I wanted to spend time with my parents, I needed to do better with spending time with Treasure. I spent the rest of the afternoon bonding with Treasure and making memories that I would cherish for the rest of my life.

# JONAH

"Daddy, can I get some more chocolate milk, please?" Leslie asked. He was a well-mannered five-year-old child, considering all he went through with his hoe ass mom who was six feet under.

"Since you ate all of your lunch, yes you can. I am going to get you guys a cup of chocolate milk."

I got up to get the kids some chocolate milk. Brii went to get her nails done and get some time away from the kids, which was well deserved. Outside of the bumps I was going through with Brii, I was content with my life. I was thinking about opening my own business so I would be able to have that generational wealth, but I wanted to see what Brii thought first. She was used to me being home with the family full time, and I didn't want her to think that I didn't care about her having a career. On the other hand, I was selfish as fuck because I wanted to have a baby by my wife and I was thrown at how adamant Brii was about never having a kid. I could accept her not being ready right now and wanting to wait a year or so, but I couldn't accept never having a child of my own. I stepped up to the plate to help her raise her siblings and I knew that wasn't easy for her, but I made sure to do more than my fair share and make sure she knew she wasn't in this alone. Leslie technically doesn't have my blood either, but I was raising him as if he was my blood, but that didn't take away from the fact that I wanted my own biological child.

I gave the kids their chocolate milk and watched them chatter away while I was deep in thought. I always wanted to have a building of my own and have that generational wealth so my children's future kids would always be straight. I wanted to be on the level of the Jackson Brothers where their future generations would be straight. I didn't regret giving up the street life, but sometimes life was a bit boring without having a regular job to go to every day. Luca still had his law license and his own law firm that I washed my money through so the FEDS didn't start coming for my ass, but I still kept feeling like something was missing in my life besides having a child of my own. I was way too young to have a mid-life crisis, but it felt like I was having one.

"Daddy, can we go outside?" Antoinette asked and every time they called me dad, it brought tears to my eyes. I might not share blood with them, but the bond was something that would never be broken.

"Wait for me to come to watch you guys, and you will stay in front where I can see you." I grabbed their glasses and put them in the dishwasher before letting the kids go outside. I followed the kids outside and watched them play in the dirt. Antoinette was dirtier than either of the boys as she was a tomboy, and I loved it. Brii didn't care for it as much as she always wanted to dress her sister up in dresses, but she was not having it. Antoinette wanted to fit in and act like she was a little nigga.

"Jonah, why are you letting Antoinette play in the damn dirt?" Brii fussed and I gave her my famous grin.

"Hey, bae. She is just playing with her brothers, let her be. man." I shrugged my shoulders.

"What if she turns out to be gay?" Brii whispered, and I frowned at her.

"Antoinette is five years old. I doubt she has no idea about her sexual orientation at that age, but I wouldn't love her any less if she was a lesbian. Hell, I will go check out bitches with her—"

*Slap! Slap!*

Brii slapped me across the face. "Nigga, you better not even think about entertaining no hoes or train my sister to be a carpet muncher—"

"Get out my face with that shit, Brii. All you been doing is nagging and complaining lately because I asked you when we would have a baby. That is a normal question that any married couple would talk about and we have been married for two years." I mushed Brii in the head. I was still upset about the argument we had a week ago over it, and what made it worse was Brii and I never sat down like two adults and talked about it. Somewhere along the line, it felt like Brii and I stopped communicating the way that we used to and now we lived more like roommates than a young married couple.

"Don't flip this on me when we never had that conversation about having kids. You assumed I would want to have kids when you knew coming into this marriage that my siblings are a package deal. We have three wonderful and intelligent kids. Why do we need any more? They can be a handful as it is, and I honestly don't want to go back to changing diapers like we used to with Leslie," Brii replied.

"I want to experience pregnancy and childbirth with you. I want to know what it is like to have a child with my blood. I always wanted a big family, and I would never force you to become Octo Mom, but I really want at least one or two biological children. I don't understand what is so unreasonable about that, Brii."

"You don't understand that I gave up my entire childhood to help raise my siblings. I want to be able to say I can do something for Brii besides raise children and be a baby factory. I lost my entire childhood due to my mom's drug addiction and I don't want to spend my entire life raising children. I love Leslie like he is my own and I know he isn't yours biologically but I don't treat him any differently than my own siblings. I love you more than anything in this world Jonah, but—"

Brii was interrupted by the sound of a loud crash and the next thing I knew, we both looked toward the street and saw that Leslie had gotten hit by a car and was bleeding. His limp body lay in the middle of the street while the person that hit Les sped away like a bat out of hell.

"Call 911 while I check for his pulse! Please do not let Leslie be dead..."

# 6

## KLAYTON

I was a little miffed that Treasure blew me off the other night, but once she explained she had gotten into it with her brother and needed some space, I understood. Good things came to those who waited, and I knew that Treasure would eventually be mine. Right now, I had to rough this little nigga named Darnell up for thinking he could get high on the fucking supply and live to tell the tale. Darnell was this little corner boy that I allowed to run one of the traps. Problem was, my money was coming up short, and my product was disappearing. Anytime I had to come and deal with this kind of shit it was never good because I am the fucking connect now. The problem was even though I had a right- hand man to handle this kind of shit, I still liked handling snakes myself. There was nothing like putting the fear of God into a nigga that bit the hand that fed him and I get off on killing mothafuckas. Darnell gave me a sob story about his father being an alcoholic, and his mother was the breadwinner. He wanted to contribute to their household even though I did my research and found out his family is wealthy and not hurting for money. I should have killed his ass for lying about the sob story he gave me when it was clear he had money but I figured his goofy ass just wanted to be about that life. I gave him a chance to get on the winning team which turned out to be the wrong move.

"Give me one fucking reason why I shouldn't kill your ass, nigga." I spat. One thing I didn't play about was my money. Luckily, the amount of drugs he stole wasn't a large amount, but it was still enough for me to notice my money was short. He has the money to pay my ass back so he better go get it from his mother if he has to.

"I- I fucked up, man. I will get you your money, I promise—" Darnell stuttered. I caught this nigga slipping after one of his classes at USC and threw his ass in my trunk in broad daylight. Ask anyone about Klayton Jackson and they will tell you I have no fucks to give, and if twelve wants this work, they can come get it.

Something told me to kill his ass, but I was trying to mature and not kill niggas for minor petty shit. That didn't mean Darnell's ass was off the hook, though.

"You got twenty-four hours to get my shit if you don't want me to blow your SpongeBob-looking head off." I grabbed my gun and pistol-whipped his ass until he was unconscious. I picked his body up and threw his body on the side of the road before I went to pick Danielle up from Trayce's house.

"Dada!" Danielle yelled the second I walked inside Trayce and Rolonda's crib, which looked more like a mansion you would have seen on *MTV Cribs*. It was decked out to the mothafucking gods, and my brother deserved it for all the work he put in over the years.

"Hey, there goes Daddy's little girl." I picked her up and swung her in the air, and she squealed. I swear this little girl is making my ass soft, and there was nothing I wouldn't do for my baby girl. I regretted a lot of bad choices I made in my life, but I never regretted my daughter.

"What you up to, bro?" Trayce dapped me up after I put

Danielle down. His son, Matthew, ran in the room and gave me baby dap.

"There goes my little nigga!" I bragged and I could already tell Matthew was going to grow up and be a few screws short like Trayce and me.

"Stop calling my son a little nigga, Klayton," Rolonda fussed. A small smile played on the side of her lips, and she knew what time it was fucking with the Jackson family.

"You know what it is, Ro. Come on, Danielle, it is time to go home now." I grabbed my daughter's hand and Ro tapped me on the shoulder.

"Did you ask Treasure out yet?" she asked.

"Yeah I did, but she got in an argument with Luca the other night and canceled. I'm going to link up with her soon, though," I promised, and I was a man of my word. Whatever it was I wanted, I went after it and got it. I was like a dog chasing a bone.

"You know if you get serious with Treasure, Luca is going to have a problem with it? It might create issues within the family again," Ro warned.

"Luca bleeds just like I bleed. I fear no nigga and if he wants to be with the shits, then we can go to war. There is something special about Treasure that draws me to her. If it was just a sex thing, I wouldn't even be trying to pursue her, but I know that is my future wife right there," I explained, and a small smile was on Trayce and Ro's face.

"Up up, Daddy!" Matthew yelled at Trayce. Trayce picked his son up and gave him a piggyback ride.

"Oh shit. I never thought I would see the day that you fall in love again, Klayton. It is good to see you vulnerable and allowing another woman in again." Ro smiled. Ro has been worried about me since all of the shit with my ex-girlfriend Shae went down

"Yo, a nigga is not in love yet. I have strong feelings for Treasure and I do want to pursue whatever this is between us, but it is a little too soon to say love." I almost wanted to pull back because it scared me how I felt about a woman I really haven't seen much in the last three years. When I met Treasure there was such a strong force between us, and even though we lost contact for three years I compared every bitch I laid pipe to Treasure and even moaned her name out a time or two. I ended up having to yoke up a crying thot up once or twice for getting in her feelings.

"Bro, let me tell you, every woman isn't going to be as toxic as Shae was. Treasure is a good woman and deep down, you know that because that is why you are trying to pursue her so hard."

"What should I do? I don't want to see you so pressed or thirsty over her and scare her away. I also don't want to cause any friction with her brother, but I will go toe to toe with him if I have to."

"What you need to do is show Treasure that you are what she needs in her life, and that you will protect her. She only knows you through us, and that hasn't been much because we are never around each other at the same time. You need to romance her and I know you have it in you, Klayton. At one time, you were kind of romantic with Shae," Ro reminded me. Shae had made me soft once upon a time but not as soft as Treasure was making me now.

"Yeah, I just don't want to be this soft ass nigga, although Treasure can break a nigga all the way down. A nigga was getting high on my shit earlier and I didn't off his ass because I felt sorry for him—"

Ro and Trayce looked at me like I was crazy. "Nigga, you know that shit gonna come back to haunt you, right? He isn't going to pay you back that money he owes you and hell, he might become an informant on your ass."

"Naw man, that little nigga knows better if he values his life…"

# HOPE GLOVER

Giovanni squeezed my hand as Dr. Henry Schulman came into the office. I knew Giovanni meant to reassure me, but at this point, nothing would make me feel comfortable until we found out whether Genesis would qualify for the corneal transplant surgery.

"Mr. and Mrs. Glover? It is good to see you guys again, and I know this is a trying time for you. I had my nurse run a panel of tests on Genesis, and I sat down and analyzed the results and would like to speak with you guys about the results. Do you guys have any questions for me?" Dr. Schulman asked.

A couple of days ago, we brought Genesis in to see the ophthalmologist, and they ran a series of tests and discovered Genesis' blood type, which was important in finding a set of donor eyes that would be a match for her. I prayed that everything was going to work out in our favor. Luca wanted to come with us, but we needed him to watch Genesis and if he came, Treasure would suspect that something was up.

"Can you just tell us whether Genesis will be eligible for the surgery or not, please? My wife and I can't take not knowing much longer," Giovanni stated impatiently.

"I understand, sir. Let me explain how this procedure works. In order to find a set of donor eyes, we would either need a dead relative's eyes or someone that has the same blood type as Genesis. We found out Genesis' blood type is AB, so we would need to find a set of donor eyes with the same blood type. The good news is, Genesis is an excellent candidate for the surgery. With your permission, I would like to add her to the wait list for the donor eye." Dr. Schulman smiled.

I had tears in my eyes as I realized my grandbaby might finally get her vision back and be able to see again. "Of course, we give you permission! How long will the wait be for the donor eye?"

"The bad news is AB is one of the rarest blood types, so it might take us some time to get a match for Genesis. We will be doing a corneal transplant, and she will be hospitalized a minimum of two days after the procedure is done. The procedure itself should take approximately two hours, and I will be sewing in her new cornea. I will have Genesis sedated to lessen the amount of pain she might feel. The procedure is different in children than it is in adults, and corneal implants usually aren't recommended for children very often. However, after looking over Genesis' case and how she developed vision problems, I feel that this is the best fit for her. She will have to wear an eye patch for a few days, and she will have to come back into the office to get the patch removed."

"Why not just keep her in the hospital for a week if the patch will be removed that quickly?" Giovanni asked. I was wondering the same thing.

"I can keep her hospitalized, but this type of surgery is typically an outpatient surgery for adults. When I do this procedure on a child, I usually hospitalize them for a couple of days and then have the patch removed in my office. It can help with their recovery if they are in familiar settings instead of being laid up in a hospital. I see here that you guys have private insurance, so even if you wanted to extend Genesis hospital stay, it wouldn't be a problem."

"Dr. Schulman, it wouldn't be a problem even if I had to pay out of pocket. Money is not an issue, and we are willing to do whatever is in the best interest of Genesis. What risks are associated with the surgery?" I asked. I played no games over the well-being of my family, and I felt Giovanni squeezing my hand.

"There is a small risk that Genesis could reject the donor eye. I will be using eye drops that will lessen the risk of the donor eye being rejected," Dr. Schulman explained.

"Why would it reject the eye if the eye is a perfect match for Genesis?" I asked.

"Simply put, it can be as simple as Genesis' immune system rejecting the tissue. Sometimes, it happens right away but in rare cases, it can happen months or years after the transplant. I don't want you guys going into this blind without knowing all of the risks. I believe the risks are worth the potential reward, especially since her vision was blurred from an STD she had gotten from birth. Since I am doing a corneal transplant on both eyes, the risk of rejection is higher," Dr. Schulman explained patiently. I could tell he felt bad for our situation, and I appreciated his honesty.

"Are there any other risks that we need to be aware of?" Giovanni asked.

"There is a risk of bleeding and infection. Swelling is a possibility as well. The biggest risk, in my opinion, is the tissue being rejected. I know this is a big decision that you guys need to make, and feel free to take the time that you need to decide. You guys have my phone number if you guys decide to go through with the surgery. Do you have any other questions?"

I looked at Giovanni, and there were a lot of thoughts running through my mind. How would we make this decision? Would we involve Treasure in making this decision, or was this something she shouldn't have to worry about?

"Thank you so much, Dr. Schulman, for your help. My wife

and I will be in touch with our decision." Giovanni led me out of the office, and we walked toward Luca's car in silence.

"Do you think we should tell Treasure? This is a big decision that will have to be made about Genesis, and we did promise not to make any major medical decisions without including her." I buckled my seat belt before Giovanni started driving.

"Treasure has so much going on with school that I don't want this to be a distraction. At the same time, if we decide to go through with the surgery, this is something she will find out anyway. We need to talk to her and Luca about this, and the sooner the better. I just got to develop a relationship with our kids, and I don't want this kind of a decision to tear us apart."

"Part of me doesn't want to tell her, but what are we going to do? Do we want to take a chance on Genesis' health by trying this surgery? What if we go through with it and it doesn't go as well as we want it to?" I was worried how this would affect Genesis. On the other hand, this surgery could change Genesis' life and give her the gift of being able to see.

"What if we don't go through with it and second-guess ourselves for the rest of our lives. Listen, we owe it to Treasure and Genesis to give this a try. Hell, we need to talk to Treasure and see what she thinks about this. She is going to kill us when she realizes she kept this from us," Giovanni admitted. I prayed Treasure wouldn't be too upset at us when she found out we withheld this information from her.

A few minutes later, he pulled up to Luca's house. We got out and walked inside, only to see Treasure waiting for us in the living room. I thought nothing of it and went into the kitchen to grab a bottle of water.

"Mom, were you ever going to tell me about this?" Treasure walked in the kitchen and shoved a set of papers in my face. They were papers confirming my appointment with Dr. Schulman, and I knew Giovanni and I were busted.

# 7

# BRII

I felt horrible for what happened. Jonah and I were at the hospital with Antoinette and Blake waiting for news on Leslie's condition. It felt like my entire world was caving in, and I had no idea who I could turn to because AJ wasn't here with me anymore. It was my fault because I decided to be a bitch and pick a fight with Jonah and now, Leslie was in the emergency room fighting for his life. You could feel the tension between Jonah and I, and I knew he was blaming me for the accident.

"Have you called Jonah?" I whispered tentatively. My hands had goosebumps on them, and my legs were quivering. My nerves were on a thousand because I just wanted to rewind time and change what happened. Unfortunately, life doesn't give you any do-overs, and I would have to live with the consequences. I felt so bad about what happened to Leslie, and I should have known better than to argue in front of the kids. Jonah and I always tried to make sure that we argue in private and we fight fair but lately, I had been flipping out on him. I wasn't sure why I had been acting crazy lately and I knew I needed to get it together.

"Yes."

That was the only word Jonah said to me and his veins were visibly popping out, so I knew he was angry. I couldn't remember the last time I saw him this angry, and I had to fight to keep from crying. I loved this man more than life itself, and I didn't want to lose him or Leslie.

"Jonah and Brii, have there been any updates?" Luca asked. He gave me a brotherly hug and gave Jonah dap.

"None so far. Whoever hit Leslie did a hit and run, and I think it was on purpose. Problem is, we don't have any more enemies and we left the streets alone, so I have no idea who could be coming for us."

"It could have been a drunk driver that hit him and was scared of going to jail. We don't know that it is an enemy," I suggested. Antoinette and Blake were sitting next to us watching videos on my iPad Mini.

"Shut up, Brii. I don't even want to hear your fucking voice right now. You knew I was watching the kids outside, and you had to pick a fucking fight with me. I swear, if Les doesn't make it through—"

I quickly got up and got in Jonah's face. "What are you going to do, nigga? You know as well as I do neither of us could have foreseen him running in the street and getting hit by a car. I refuse to let you blame me for this. It was an accident, asshole." Deep down, I knew the accident was my fault and I didn't need Jonah throwing it in my face.

"Maybe if you didn't pick a fucking fight, I would have seen Les running toward the street and would have been able to stop him! You are a selfish bitch—"

"Family of Leslie Lyons?" A middle-aged doctor called our name. Luca had stepped in between us.

"I will stay here with the kids. Go see what the doctor has to say," Luca instructed us, and he took a seat with Antoinette and Blake.

"I am Leslie's father. Will he be ok?" Jonah asked, and I could see how upset he was. I would do anything to take his pain away, but I couldn't.

"Leslie will be fine. He has a broken leg and a concussion, but he is a strong little boy. I would like to keep him here under observation for the concussion for the next forty-eight to seventy-two hours. If everything is all clear with his MRI's and CAT scans, then I will allow him to go home. My name is Dr. Joseline Becker, and I wish we weren't meeting under these circumstances. If you need anything, and I do mean anything, please don't hesitate to let me know." She held her hand out for Jonah to shake and instead of just shaking his hand like a professional, she embraced him in a hug that was too sexual for my liking.

*If this bitch doesn't get her hands off my husband, then she won't live to see tomorrow,* I thought to myself. I felt belittled and disrespected, and what made it worse was Jonah entertaining the shit. There is no way in hell he should have allowed the doctor to hug him especially with his wife standing right next to him. Part of me felt like he was being petty because I wouldn't have his baby.

"When can I go see my son? Will you be the doctor in charge of his care?" Jonah asked, and he was treating me like I wasn't even there standing next to him.

"You can go see him for a few minutes. Leslie is asleep and he needs to get his rest. Let me give you my business card in case you need anything." Dr. Becker batted her eyes at Jonah, and I lost my shit. I knew we weren't on good terms, but how could he entertain the next bitch in front of me?

I grabbed the bitch by her hair and started dragging her into the hospital waiting room.

"Bitch, you are going to stop flirting with my husband, with your disrespectful ass. You saw me standing next to him and didn't even address me not one fucking time." I punched the doctor in the face, and she started screaming hysterically before Jonah and a security officer got in between us.

"Yo Brii, what the fuck are you doing? Why are you cutting

the fuck up when you are the reason Leslie's ass is in the hospital? Blake and Antoinette are watching you act a fucking fool, and you are focused on some broad disrespecting you. Luca, take her ass home!" Jonah yelled angrily.

"Don't flip this shit on me, nigga. You allowing this bitch to touch on you and shit, knowing my ass standing right next to you as your fucking wife. I'm good on your ass, nigga. Don't bother coming home." I wanted to go see Leslie, but I was so angry I couldn't stand to be around my own husband right now.

"You don't ever have to worry about me coming home again because I want a divorce from your selfish ass..."

# LUCA

I was at the hospital comforting Jonah, and I knew he didn't mean it when he told Brii that he wanted a divorce.

"Bruh, you can't really blame Brii for what happened. You know as well as I do that was an accident."

"I am sick of Brii's shit, man. I gave up everything for her and put my life on the line to save her siblings. She doesn't want to have sex anymore because she is so worried about getting pregnant by me, as if that is the worst thing in the world. She shuts me down on anything concerning having a kid of my own and has been nagging lately about stupid shit. Then, she picks a fight in front of the kids, knowing we don't argue in front of the kids and Leslie gets hurt. I would have seen Leslie running in the street if she hadn't started that dumb ass argument, and now I might not get to see my son because she picked a fight with the fucking doctor." Jonah was pissed, and I understood where he was coming from.

I was about to speak, but when I saw a couple of police officers tap Jonah on the shoulder, I knew it wasn't going to be a good situation. "Excuse me, sir, we are going to have to ask you to leave the premises—"

"What the fuck? I am not leaving while my son is here. Fuck you Gumby-looking bitches, trying to kick me out of the hospital over something I didn't even do!" Jonah roared. I needed to step in quickly as things were getting ugly.

"Listen Robocop, my friend here just wants to see his son, and we aren't leaving until he gets to see Les. Are we clear?" I took charge of the situation. Dr. Becker was acting too dramatic over the punch Brii landed, acting like she broke her damn leg or something. I didn't care what anyone said, that doctor bitch knew what she was doing flirting with Jonah in front of Brii. Jonah was wrong for entertaining the shit and even threatening Brii with a divorce, and I was going to check his ass in private.

Dr. Becker had a smug look on her face. Like I said, she knew exactly what the fuck she was doing trying to stir the fucking pot.

"Listen, I can make all of your troubles go away. Give me one date and I will make sure that you don't get arrested. I would hate for your son to not get to see his father—"

I quickly yoked Dr. Becker's ass up against the wall until her face turned blue. "What the fuck is that bullshit you are spitting? Your thirsty bucket ass is not going to use Les as leverage to get my very married brother to go out with your ass. Your pussy probably drier than the Sahara Desert if you have to resort to such desperate measures to get a date," I fussed.

"Bruh, chill," Jonah began. He placed a hand on my shoulder, and I looked at his ass like he was crazy. He had no business defending this broad and he was going to lose his wife if he continued with the fuck boy behavior.

"Are you really going to defend this broad right now?" I asked Jonah. He was wrong two ways from Sunday, and I knew he was only doing this to be petty because he was mad at Brii.

"He obviously sees something he likes in me if he is defending me instead of that fat bitch—"

"Man, who the fuck gave you a medical license? I thought you are supposed to take a course on professionalism and ethics while you are in medical school," I fussed. Someone had obviously called the police on us. We had created a spectacle in the waiting room, and Dr. Becker and I both looked at Jonah to see how he was going to react.

"All of this can go away if you agree to one date with me, Jonah. If we go on one date and you never want to see me again, then I will walk away with no questions asked. You will never hear a peep out of me outside of caring for your child. What do you say?" Dr. Becker asked.

I prayed because I knew my brother was vulnerable. The last thing he needed was to fall into this skank's trap, and it was time for me to be my brother's keeper. Jonah opened his mouth to speak, but I interrupted him before he could say anything.

"Hell no. He is not going out with your desperate BENGAY pussy smelling ass. I can smell that rank ass vagina from here. Your ass needs to clean that shit."

"Well, I guess Jonah would rather see his wife go to jail than go on a date with me. Officers, I would like to press charges on his wife that assaulted me. She looks like an Amazon-looking bitch." Dr. Becker smiled and I was fuming.

"Well, I guess you wouldn't mind me reporting your ass to the state board for violating the ethics code, hoe. Little did you know, I got your ass recorded on camera." I pulled my phone out, and it had recorded everything she had been saying.

"It is illegal to record in the state of California without having my consent, so they will throw that shit out in court." Dr. Becker's thirsty ass waved me away.

Jonah looked like he was stuck in between a rock and a hard place. It should have been a no brainer what he was going to do, and I would always ride behind my brother. What scared me was the reality that he was really considering going out on a date with the doctor.

"Jonah, you need to check this bitch, man. What she is doing is foul and you know it," I called my bruh out. I was really worried because he was going to lose Brii with the way he was acting.

"It might be foul, but there isn't a bitch alive that will come before my son."

# 8

# TREASURE

"Mom, what is this? I thought we agreed that all medical decisions for Genesis would be made together. This looks like an appointment for an ophthalmologist that does special eye surgeries. Why do I feel like there is something you guys aren't telling me?" I asked with my arms folded across my breasts.

"Treasure, sit down, honey. Let me explain. I didn't want you to find out this way." My mom pleaded, and she had tears in her eyes. I wasn't moved by those tears, even when my father came into the room. My hands were trembling and I felt betrayed by those that were supposed to be loyal to me.

"Treasure, go have a seat and we will talk about this in the living room." My father ordered, and I stood still. I felt betrayed because I never thought my parents would keep any more secrets from me. I understood the reason my father had abandoned us in the past and therapy helped me get past that, but this was a betrayal involving my daughter. In a weird way, I felt like they were trying to replace Luca and me with Genesis because they never got to raise us together as a family unit.

"No. What I need is an answer to my question, Dad. I thought we were better than this. You guys kept a huge secret about my daughter's health, and I am demanding answers!" I screamed at the top of my lungs. The next thing I knew, my mom had slapped me across the face.

*Whap! Whap!*

I stood there frozen because I couldn't believe my mother put her hands on me. Hell, I disrespected her a lot worse when I was younger and she didn't put her hands on me the way she just did. I felt violated and disrespected, like my feelings were not important.

"Treasure, I am sorry! I didn't mean to put my hands on you, baby girl. I just feel like you only want to claim Genesis as your daughter when it is convenient for you. Your father and I have had to do the job of raising her and making tough decisions. We aren't perfect by any means but I will be damned if you disrespect us. Please come back!" my mom called.

I ran back to my room in tears and grabbed my cell phone and car keys. Then, I ran and made sure Genesis was still asleep before I headed out to my car. I didn't even bother putting on my seat belt as I raced out of there like a bat out of hell before my parents could catch me. I placed my Bluetooth in my ear, and I was going to call Rolonda or Brii but my phone started ringing and I saw it was Klayton. I felt butterflies in my stomach as I answered the call.

"Hey, Klayton. What's up?" I answered nonchalantly.

"Hey, Treasure. I have been thinking about you, and I wanted to reach out to you to see when we could go on that date."

"I am available now and can drive to you. I am already in my car, and I have no idea where I am going," I admitted. I needed to get away from my family before I said something to my parents that I would end up regretting later.

"What's wrong? Baby girl, it sounds like you are crying. Hell, pull over at Magic Johnson Park and I will meet you there in thirty minutes. I already know you are not too far off from there as I put a tracker on your phone the day I ran into you at Starbucks. Just go and wait for me there. I just have to get Danielle ready and I will be there soon," Klayton ordered. He definitely wasn't the type of man that I wanted to try to check because I knew his ass was with the shits.

"Klayton, I am fine—"

"Don't argue with me, Treasure. I already know you are lying. I will see you in thirty minutes and remember, if you don't show up, I will show up to your house and wait until you show up." Klayton's crazy ass hung up on me, and I shook my head at his crazy ass. There was something about this man that was drawing me in, and I wanted to know more about him. I knew better than to go against his orders especially if I didn't want shit to hit the fan if Luca saw him pop up at our house.

I arrived at the park a few minutes later and parked my car. I sat down to my thoughts, and maybe I was overreacting about Genesis's doctor appointment. When we all went to family therapy a couple of years ago, I made it clear I didn't like secrets and couldn't deal with any secrets coming out of the woodwork. I failed to understand why my parents would keep such a big secret from me, especially considering that they knew I had been trying to build a relationship with my daughter.

I heard Klayton knock on my car window, and he had startled my ass. I jumped and then realized it was him standing there alone. I opened my car door confused.

"Where is Danielle at?" I asked.

"I dropped her off with Trayce and Rolonda on the way here. I figured you needed a friend and someone to talk to. We can talk here if you want, or we can go to my house where it is more private. Don't worry, I am not going to try anything sexual with you. You look like you can use a friend and I want to be there for you." Klayton looked sincere and I wondered out of all the women he could go get, why me?

"Why me, Klayton? I know there are plenty of women that would love to have you and come with less baggage—"

"Ssshhh, Treasure. There is something about you that draws me in, and I want to get to know you better. I have had my own baggage in the past, and that shit wears you down. I know that you have been hurt, Treasure, because looking at you is like looking at a reflection of myself. I don't need to spit game at you because if I wanted pussy, we both know I could pick the hoe up from down the street and get it. I am too old to keep sharing my dick with every bitch in the streets, and if I want different then I need to move differently, and I am trying to do that with you. What do you say?" Klayton, asked and he stared straight through my soul.

For some reason, I didn't hesitate with Klayton like I would with other men. There was a protective aura surrounding him and I instinctively trusted him, which was hard considering my past with men.

"You know what? That sounds good. I could use a friend right now. Let me follow you to your house in my car."

# KLAYTON

"Make sure you get comfortable. I picked up all of Danielle's toys earlier. Do you want anything to drink?" I asked politely. I knew Treasure was special because she had me moving differently than I would with other women. Shit, even Shae used to get my hoe treatment in the past and, for some reason, I didn't want to give Treasure that same treatment. She deserved better, and I was the man that was going to give it to her.

"Do you have anything to eat? I am hungry." Treasure rubbed her tummy.

"I have some stuff, but I am not the greatest cook in the world. I am sure I can whip us up some spaghetti. It is hard to burn spaghetti. Give me a few minutes and I will cook that up, if that is okay."

"How in the hell do you not know how to cook and you are a single father? Please don't tell me you are feeding Danielle McDonald's every day." Treasure put her hands on her small, yet curvy hips. I licked my lips at the thought of her riding my dick, but I knew my attraction to Treasure was more than physical. I normally didn't like women as young as Treasure, but I felt a strong pull toward her.

"Naw, but my sis Ro normally cooks extra and gives me enough to last Danielle and me most of the week. Then the other days, we order pizza or eat out. I need to learn how to cook more than spaghetti and waffles. Can you teach me, beautiful?" I flirted with Treasure and she blushed. I knew she was feeling the kid, and I wanted her to feel safe with me. When I looked into her eyes, I could see a lot of pain in them and I wanted to know everything about her.

"Nigga, let me in that kitchen before you fuck up our spaghetti. I got this, Klayton," Treasure fussed and sashayed into the kitchen. I saw her digging through kitchen cabinets shaking her head. She started pulling out ingredients to make the spaghetti, and I decided to try to make a salad.

I grabbed the ingredients to make the vegetable salad, but it looked like the vegetables had wilted. "I was going to at least make a salad, but umm, the lettuce went bad."

"Klayton, you could not have thought you could use these spaghetti noodles. They have weevils in them. You really need me to go grocery shopping for you and get you into shape. Your daughter deserves better than this, and your spaghetti sauce had an expiration date from two years ago," Treasure complained.

I was embarrassed because I had no idea the stuff had gone bad already. "My bad, and I never would expose my daughter to that. I would have thrown it out when I tried to cook it. How about we order some pizza?"

"That works. Later, you need to take me grocery shopping for you. Hell, I will start cooking your meals so I know Danielle is getting fed properly. You are not living the bachelor lifestyle anymore, and as long as we are friends,, I am going to make sure you are good," Treasure fussed.

I pressed my body against hers and whispered in her ear. "Are you sure we are just friends, Treasure? I think you know as well as I do that there is something more brewing between us."

"Klayton, all we can be is friends right now. My brother—" Treasure tried protesting.

"Don't worry about your brother. Let me handle him. Luca bleeds just as much as I do. When we make things official, I have no problem having that heart to heart talk with Luca and if he wants to take it there with me, then he can." I shrugged my shoulders. I lifted Treasure's chin to meet mine and I kissed her gently on the lips and she tasted good. I slid my tongue inside her mouth and she wrapped her small frame around my big body. I felt my rod bricking up in my pants, and it was taking everything in me to restrain myself.

I finally broke the kiss and Treasure had left me stuck on stupid. I could tell that I had a similar effect on her, and it felt good to know that a nigga still had it. This was beyond mere physical attraction, and I knew this woman was going to be my wife one day. I could see my entire future in her eyes, and I wanted to take the pain away from whoever hurt her in the past.

"Klayton, I shouldn't have kissed you—"

"Sssh. That was all me and I wanted it as much as you did. I won't push you to do anything you aren't ready to do. I do want to get to know you better, Treasure. Grab something to drink and I am going to order the pizza. What toppings do you want on your pizza?" I asked.

"Pepperoni and extra cheese, please, and some cheese sticks. Please order Pizza Hut. Their pizza is the best." Treasure's smile lit up the entire room, and I would do anything to make her happy. Domino's tastes like an old ass cardboard box anyways so I was more than happy to order Pizza Hut.

"Go get comfortable in the living room, and the control to the parental control is eight-three-one-one. Find us something to watch while I go order our meal."

I left Treasure to go order our pizza, which took less than ten minutes. My phone went off and I saw a notification on Facebook from some broad named Barbara who continued sending me

DMs from fake profiles. She had been trying to get the dick for over a year, but she was way too pressed and thirsty. Once I became a single father, I changed my lifestyle around because my daughter deserved to have all attention on her. There was no need for me to live the lifestyle of a single man when I needed to be a positive example to Danielle on how a man is supposed to treat a woman. It was bad enough I was still giving that other bitch dick occasionally but little did she know she was getting cut off.

"Hey, did you have a hard time with the TV?" I asked Treasure. I walked to the couch she was sitting on and took a seat next to hers.

"No, I just thought we could talk. I can watch TV at home, but I want to know more about you, Klayton. When we met three years ago, I was attracted to you then, but the timing was all bad. I went through so much shit that I went to therapy for, and I still go at least once a month just to work on myself."

"What do you want to know? I am an open book and I want you to be able to trust me." I sat right next to Treasure and she smelled delectable.

"Where is your baby momma? It is hard for me to believe that you are single like you claim and you aren't smashing your baby momma. I have a lot of trust issues, Klayton, and haven't dated in years. If I decide to invest in spending time with you and pursuing a relationship with you, I am going to want to know that the risk is worth the reward," Treasure explained. I could smell the cherry blossom perfume that she had on, and it smelled so good on her that I would go and buy out *Bath and Body Works* just to always smell that on her.

"Tabitha died not long after giving birth to Danielle. My bitter ex-girlfriend snuck into her hospital room and smothered her with a pillow—"

"Klayton, I am sorry. I didn't mean to pry." Treasure placed her hand over her mouth. Honestly, I was glad she asked that question so we could get it out of the way. I didn't want her to worry about my baby mother because obviously, she wouldn't be a factor.

"No, don't worry about it. Tabitha's mother tried to sue me to get custody of my daughter and luckily, I managed to win custody. I still allow her to see her grandparents once a month, at least. Tabitha's parents are the only set of grandparents Danielle has since my parents are dead. I just want you to see that I am a single father, but you don't have to worry about the typical baby momma drama with me." I never explained myself to any woman in the past the way I was explaining myself to Treasure. I don't know if this was just a change from me maturing, or if it was because Treasure was a different breed of woman than what I was used to dealing with.

"Do you get along with her parents? Is that a messy situation?" Treasure asked curiously.

"Her mother hates me and blames me for Tabitha's death. We have an arranged pick-up situation at a police station where Tabitha's brother Mitchell picks her up and brings her back to me. I wish we could bury the hatchet for Danielle's sake, but she blames me for her daughter's death and in a way, she is right. I should have protected her from Shae because Shae was showing crazy tendencies at the time," I admitted.

"Wait, are you talking about the same bitch that killed AJ?" Treasure asked as she put the pieces together, and I nodded my head in response.

"Shae kept trying to get back with me, but our relationship had always been toxic. At one point, I thought I was in love with her, but we kept bringing the worst out in each other. It came to a point where I realized that we were no good for each other, and for a while, she agreed and kept her distance. I found out after Shae and AJ died that she was diagnosed with bipolar disorder and stopped taking her medication, and I kept blaming myself. I should have done more."

Treasure wrapped her small arms around me and it felt good.

"Klayton, you didn't know and nothing about that situation was your fault. I know Luca used to blame you for what happened to AJ, but Shae refused to accept the help that she needed. There was nothing you could have done, Klayton, and I need you to understand that."

"I know there was nothing I could have done differently. It still feels like a bad D-rated movie that plays in my head occasionally, but I am grateful that Danielle has at least one of her parents here to raise her. Now, what had you upset earlier?" I really wanted to help Treasure work through whatever issues she was going through, and I could tell that she had a lot on her mind.

"Well, my parents made a major medical decision with my daughter without discussing it with me first—"

"Wait, you have a daughter?" I completely forgot that Treasure had a child, and I was curious to know more about their situation. I prayed she wasn't a deadbeat parent because I would lose interest in her and drop her lack a sack of potatoes real quick.

"Yes, her name is Genesis and she is four years old. My situation is really deep, though, and—"

"Treasure, I am a single father. If anyone can understand and try to relate to you, it would be me. Do you feel comfortable telling me?" I asked. Treasure took a second but gave me a head nod, and I had no idea at how deep her story was.

"Genesis was conceived by rape. I don't know if you remember that evil cop, Blach, but he had been raping me for months and he got me pregnant. I tried to get an abortion at the time and the situation didn't work out that way. When I gave birth to Genesis, Blach had given me gonorrhea but I didn't know it because I didn't have symptoms from an STD. She was born fully blind due to that piece of shit," Treasure spat and she had tears in her eyes. It was my turn to comfort her now.

"I wish I could bring his ass back from the dead and kill that piece of shit again. You didn't deserve what happened to you, Treasure, and Genesis deserved a better fate than she got. I admire your strength because you are in school and you are raising a child with a disability? You are stronger than you give yourself credit for." I tipped my cap to Treasure as she had been through more than women twice her age.

"Thank you. Honestly, I have a lot of help and I can't take all of the credit. After everything happened three years ago, I allowed my parents to take full custody of Genesis so I could finish school and be able to give my daughter a better life eventually. I want to be independent and stand on my own two feet because my family has been super supportive since I gave birth to Genesis. She deserves the world, and I plan to give it to her. I won't lie, it was hard for a while to even bond with her because of the circumstances surrounding her conception. I love her more than life itself though, and I went through what I went through for a reason." Treasure's strength shone through, and I knew at that moment I was already falling for her. I vowed to get her in a position where she could regain custody of her daughter.

# 9

# TREASURE

I found myself losing track of time talking to Klayton and opening myself up to him in ways I never expected on our first impromptu date. It wasn't the fanciest of dates, but a woman like me didn't need that and Klayton knew it. We spent all evening talking, and I was relieved when we started talking about more light-hearted topics. We spent time actually connecting and I could tell he has a heart of gold. The look on his face when I told him my story was a look of a lion wanting to protect his cub and it felt good to have someone that wasn't family feel that way about me.

"What is your favorite color, Treasure?" Klayton asked.

"Yellow, because it represents sunshine and happiness. I have seen so much darkness in my life that when I see the color yellow, it reminds me of positivity. Sunflowers are my favorite flowers because they are yellow and represent happiness," I explained.

Klayton was holding me in his big strong arms, and I felt so secure there. I couldn't remember ever having a man take a romantic interest in me that wasn't just sexual. When I was in high school, I had classmates that wanted to hit, but it was always shallow and they never really got to know the real Treasure.

"I love the color blue. When I was younger, I had blue everything in my room and Trayce used to clown me for it. What is your favorite food?" Klayton asked.

"My favorite food is lasagna and garlic bread. And I am not talking about the shit you get at Olive Garden. I can make a killer homemade lasagna," I bragged.

"You need to show me your kitchen skills one day. And yes, I will take you grocery shopping but you gotta let me take you on a real date first. I want to show you how a man treats a woman." Klayton was staring at me like he wanted to eat me alive, and I was surprisingly horny. My panties were wet just looking at Klayton, and I couldn't remember the last time I had been turned on. I wanted to jump his bones, but I knew it was too soon.

"Honestly, this is an amazing first date. I am really enjoying have the chance to chop it up with you and get to know you. When everything went down years ago, you struck me as a man that is that protector and will give his all for the ones he cares about. I was attracted to you then and it scared me, but I also heard how shit went down with you and Luca and I knew it was best to leave things alone back then," I admitted.

"Listen, Luca and I let the beef go years ago. I know when he finds out we are seeing each it other, it might create some tension or drama but know that I fear no one, including your brother. You have to be willing to fight for us if we are going to make this relationship work." Klayton took a sip of his beer.

"I feel you, but he doesn't like the idea of me dating anyone. When we were supposed to go out the other night, he was upset at the thought of me going on a date period. I know it would be even worse if he knew I was going out with you, even though you guys squashed your beef. Luca has been very overprotective of me since everything went down, and it is even worse since I moved in with him to finish school. I wanted to get my own apartment, but Luca wasn't having it and my parents weren't either."

"They just want to be able to protect you, Treasure. You went through so much and I can understand why they are all so protective of you. I get that you want more space, though. Luca might have run every other nigga that wanted to date you off, but he won't run me off. That is a promise."

"I don't want it to cause any more conflict, especially since you guys buried the hatchet. I know you guys won't ever be close, but I do want you guys to get along," I whispered. I knew it was a bad idea that I wanted to date Klayton because this would cause drama within my family, but the heart wants what the heart wants.

"I have no beef with Luca, and I can understand why he felt the way he felt. I also won't be a secret, so if we decide this is something that we want to do, then know that I am going to him man to man as well as to your father to let them know what it is. I am not one of these fraudulent niggas out in these streets that won't go to war, and I am prepared to fight for you, Treasure."

I had tears in my eyes. I could tell Klayton wasn't just running game on me just to get in my pants. He had feelings developing for me and it scared me. I have never experienced what it was like to be in love and only really saw my parents in love, and Luca when he fell for AJ. Part of me was scared of the way love broke Luca down because if that was love, honey, I didn't want any parts of it.

"I just know it won't end well—" Before I could finish my statement, my phone started ringing and it startled me. I saw it was my father and I sent him to voicemail.

"Why didn't you answer the phone for your father?" Klayton asked. He saw it was my dad on the caller ID.

"Honestly, I need space from them for the moment. I got home from class and relieved the babysitter that was watching Genesis. Like I told you before, we have a legally binding agreement that while they have physical custody of Genesis, that I am included in all of the major medical decisions for her. If I decide in the future that I am prepared to raise her on my own—"

"Not if, you mean when," Klayton corrected me. There was something about him that made me want to be better for my daughter, and I had a feeling he was going to get me all the way together. The thing was, I needed to get myself together and not for him but for Genesis because she deserves it.

"Yeah, don't get me wrong. I am not superficial and it doesn't scare me off that my daughter is blind. I just want to be in the position where I can provide for all of her wants and needs. Genesis deserves the world, and I am going to give it to her. I also know working as a therapist won't make me a millionaire, but I am going to tell you something I never told anyone."

"What is that?" Klayton was hanging on to every word that I said. It felt good to know that someone other than my therapist was really listening to me and taking my feelings into consideration. "I always wanted to write a book about what I went through and share my experience with others. It isn't even about making money off the book, but knowing that what I went through can help someone else would make it all worth it. If I can help expose police brutality as well, that is an added bonus. I was a teenager when Blach raped me and I had Genesis. I wasn't ready to raise a child, let alone one diagnosed with a disability. I am finally getting myself in a position where I will be emotionally and financially secure enough to take care of my daughter. I don't want to have to ask my brother to give me money for any medical stuff Genesis needs. I won't take full custody of her until I know I can take care of her on my own two feet," I explained.

Klayton looked impressed. "I support what you are trying to do and anything I can do, I got you. You are different than these hoes out here just looking for a fucking come up. I agree with your family on focusing on your education because you are about to change people's lives with your testimony. You will be able to empathize with those that have been through the same thing and be able to help them on a more personal level. Now, back to what you were telling me. Why didn't you answer your phone for your dad? Remember, life is too short for petty arguments, and there was a point in time you thought your mother was dead three years ago," Klayton reminded me.

"Well, my parents took Genesis to get checked out by an ophthalmologist and I had no idea about it. Those are the doctors that do special eye surgeries, so they must have been looking into possible surgeries for Genesis to help restore her vision. We agreed when they took custody of Genesis that I would be included in all major medical decisions, and I didn't like the fact that they kept this a secret from me. I have had enough lies and bullshit to last me a lifetime," I admitted reluctantly. Part of me felt like they were pushing me out of Genesis life and I really didn't fit in it at all anymore.

"Do you think they didn't tell you because they wanted to hurt you, or maybe they didn't want to get your hopes up until they knew more about the possibility of the eye surgery? Remember, you are their daughter and they have seen you hurt more than any parent would ever want to see their child hurt. That had to have played a part in their decision. Maybe they were going to sit down and talk to you if it became more of a reality," Klayton suggested.

What he was saying did make a lot of sense and I didn't agree with it, but I guess I could understand it. "I would probably be the same way over Genesis and that probably is what it is. My issue is I don't like big things like that being kept from me, regardless of the reason. Deep down, I feel guilty because Genesis knows me as her sister and not as her mother."

"We need to do something about that, and the first step is to help you get more involved in your daughter's life."

# JONAH

Brii had me fucked up putting me in this position. I knew it was petty to agree to this date,, knowing that the doctor was acting unprofessional, but I wanted to do this to show Brii that she didn't run my ass. I was ignoring the doctor because I had every intention of reporting the doctor after visiting my son, and I still might because this bitch wasn't going to get over on me. After I agreed to go on the date, I was able to go back and visit Les, and he was awake but drowsy. I spent about an hour with him before he was falling asleep, and I promised to come back to visit him tomorrow. Meanwhile, I was going home to grab some clothes and go get a hotel room. I made plans to meet up with Dr. Becker at Olive Garden at eight p.m. The dumb doctor thought she was doing something, but I had a plan for her ass and she was going to lose her job.

I pulled up to my house and walked inside to see Antoinette and Blake playing.

"Daddy!" they screamed. They knew I wasn't their father but since I was the closest thing to a father that they knew, they called me daddy and it made me feel good knowing I had such an impact on their lives. No matter what happened with my marriage, I would always be here for them.

"Hey, are you guys being good for Brii?" I asked them. They looked at Brii like a mother figure but also knew that was their sister.

"Yes, she made us chicken and waffles and let us watch *Frozen* and *Toy Story*." Blake smiled. Antoinette held her arms out for me to give her a piggyback ride and no matter how big she got, I would oblige. They came a long way from the scrawny kids that we rescued from Romano's evil hands.

"Jonah, can we talk for a minute, please? I left you a plate of food in the microwave." Brii walked in the room, and my dick started bricking up in my pants. There would never be another woman that I would desire the way I wanted Brii. Her behavior lately had frustrated me, but I loved the shit out of her.

I didn't feel like talking to her, but I also didn't feel like risking her cutting up in front of the kids. "Give me a minute. I will meet you in the kitchen." I dismissed Brii.

She stared at me for a minute. "Fine, nigga." She walked off and I told the kids to go play in their bedrooms before I went in the kitchen.

I grabbed my plate out of the microwave and sniffed it a couple of times. My wife Brii was very petty, and I put nothing past her. I needed to be sure that she didn't put anything in my damn food.

"Brii, they almost didn't let me go back there and see Les because of what you pulled on that doctor. I am not saying she wasn't foul, but I was going to handle that shit by reporting her ass to the state later on." I took a bite out of the food Brii prepared and it was delicious. It was almost enough to make me let go of my anger toward her, but not quite.

"Listen. I'm sorry Jonah, but I couldn't stand back and let that bitch flirt with my husband. You know you would have been mad if that situation was reversed." Brii had a point, but I also would have handled it differently. Shit, I might have blown the nigga's head off in broad daylight.

"Yes, but I also wouldn't have picked a fight and beat her ass. Shit, you should have blown her head off or let the shit rock. You know damn well I would have handled it, and I never gave you a reason to be insecure. There is nothing that bucktooth ass doctor got that I want because I love my women with meat on their bones. That way, when I'm giving your ass back shots, I can pull your hair while hitting it from the back."

I felt the tension in the room start to lessen and Brii smiled. "Nigga, you are crazy. I love you, Jonah, and I apologize for over-reacting. I am not for disrespect and that bitch was trying me. I know that you wouldn't cheat on me, but I have been a bit inse-cure lately."

I gestured for Brii to sit on my lap, and she did as she was told. I held her close to me. "What is going on with you, Brii? Is it something I am doing wrong? I love you and we are a team. I can't fix it if I don't know what is wrong."

Tears slid down Brii's face, and I started kissing her tears away. I would give up my life for hers with no questions asked. "It is nothing you did. I know that you want kids of your own, and I am scared you will cheat on me with the next bitch and get her pregnant because I don't want kids."

Part of me was insulted that Brii would even think that, but I understood where her mind was going. It was my job as her husband to make her feel secure in her position.

"Brinisha Lyons, there is not another woman out there that can hold a candle to you. Yes, I would love to have a biological child with you, and this is something we should have discussed before we got married. Honestly, I still would have married you even if I knew you never wanted to have a child of your own. I fell in love with your kind, compassionate spirit. You are beautiful, smart, intelligent and the entire fucking package. There is nothing another woman can give me that will compare to you. Do you understand?"

Brii stared lovingly into my eyes. "I love you so much and I am so sorry, Jonah. Please forgive me. I know what happened to Leslie was my fault and—"

"Sssh. That was an accident and I owe you an apology too, Brii. I never should have disrespected you with what I said to you at the hospital. I was angry and I didn't mean to hurt your feelings. We do need to do better about arguing in front of the kids, but neither of us expected Leslie to run in the street chasing his ball, and part of me thinks that hit and run might be on purpose," I admitted. I was confused on who would have did it because I left the street life alone a long time ago.

"Who the fuck would try to hit an innocent kid on purpose? I think it might have been a drunk driver." Brii frowned.

"If someone did hit Les on purpose, it will come out and I will go back to being that savage ass nigga because you know I don't play over my family." I retired from the streets three years ago, but my ass would easily go back if my families' lives were at risk.

"Jonah Cane is retired and I really want it to stay that way. We are supposed to be living our best lives right now and enjoying raising our families together. Hell, we were talking about starting a business and I really want to open a clothing store. You know I am great with fashion." Brii smiled and I was happy to see her smiling again.

"You can have whatever you like, Brii baby," I sang and Brii was laughing at me. The next thing I knew, she had my dick in her hand and she was stroking it. Then, she started fucking me with her mouth and I felt like I died and went to heaven. I busted quite a few nuts in her mouth before she pulled her pants down and started riding my hard, long tool.

I swear, every time Brii and I fucked, it felt like it was the first time we ever had sex. Her wet treasure box was sucking me in, and there was no way in hell I was going to be able to pull out.

"Damn Jonah, I'm gonna cum," Brii announced, and she continued bouncing up and down on my rod. Her big, juicy titties were bouncing right in front of my face and I ripped her shirt and bra off. I eagerly grabbed one of her boobs and started sucking on it, and I knew it wasn't going to be much longer before we both climaxed.

We finished our impromptu sex session, and our kitchen smelled like sex.

"Get your ass on the counter and spread your legs wide open, Brii," I demanded. She looked at me like I was crazy.

"Nigga, I am a big girl and I don't want to fall," Brii whined.

"Don't make me have to take you to the fucking chamber and punish you, Brii," I ordered.

Brii quickly got with the program because she didn't want to go to the chamber. The chamber was a room I used to punish Brii when she was misbehaving. A year and a half ago, Brii and I got into some S&M shit and it really spiced up our sex life, even though it had never been boring.

I watched her climb on the counter and spread her legs open. I quickly went to town feasting on her clit, and I bent her legs back. Brii was very flexible and she tasted better than the cranberry sauce that the hoes that can't cook bring to Thanksgiving dinner.

"Jonahhhhh! I love you, baby!" Brii moaned in my ear, and I could feel myself getting hard again. Once we got the kids to bed, I swore I was going to go rounds with my wife tonight. I continued licking her clit and lost track of how long I was buried between her legs. My phone started ringing, and Brii got to my phone before I could get it.

"Hello?" Brii answered.

"Is Jonah there? This is Joseline calling and we are supposed to be meeting up tonight." I heard the good ole thirsty doctor's voice come through the phone, and I immediately knew that my ass was back in trouble with my wife.

# 10

## GIOVANNI

"Have you called Treasure again?" Hope asked. She was biting her nails, which was something she did whenever she got upset.

"Yeah, she isn't answering the phone and she has been gone for hours. I am about to go looking for her. I don't want to call Luca and worry him, but I have no idea where Treasure would go when she is upset." I was pacing back and forth and deep in thought.

"I told you it was a bad idea to keep this from Treasure. I knew she would be upset with us, but I didn't expect her to react this badly." Hope cried. I walked over to her and wrapped my arms around her.

"We will find her and we will make things right. Trust me, babe. I need you to stay and watch Genesis. I will call you as soon as I know anything. Keep calling Treasure and if you get ahold of her, tell her to come home," I ordered.

"Okay, baby. Be careful. I need you to come home in one piece. I love you, Gio." Hope kissed me passionately and I wanted to make love to my wife. I needed to go find my daughter and bring her home in one piece. I reluctantly broke the kiss and grabbed the car keys before I headed to leave the house. I was just about to open the front door when the door opened and Luca entered.

"Hey, where are you going, Dad?" Luca asked. He looked exhausted, and I could tell he had a long day.

"I gotta go find your sister. Your mom and I got in a fight earlier with Treasure, and she left and hasn't been home since—"

"Let's go. I'm going with you, Pops, and I got a tracking device on her phone so I can trace her location. I always had that for her safety so I could find her. Don't tell me she found out about the ophthalmologist appointment." Luca looked at me expectantly.

I hated that I felt like I owed my son an explanation, but I lost out on my chance to be able to raise him and for him to be able to talk to me any kind of way. At the end of the day, I was still his father and deserved respect.

"Yeah, and she went off on us but I was trying to protect her feelings in case this didn't pan out. We are wasting time. Track her location," I ordered. Luca locked the front door and turned the alarm on before we got in his car.

"I will drive, Pops, you look like you had a long day. I just got a location. What the fuck is she doing at that nigga Klayton Jackson's house? Oh hell the fuck naw!" Luca roared. My son looked like he was about to have a heart attack and I needed to find a way to calm him down.

"Luca, let me drive, you are not in the right state of mind to be driving—"

"Pops, you can get in or call an Uber but my ass is driving, and he better not be fucking my little sister. Either way, that nigga Klayton got an ass whooping coming to him." Luca's veins were popping and he was pissed to the extreme.

I knew there was no calming my son down when he got this mad, so I decided to hop in the passenger seat and pray to God. Luca sped off like a bat out of hell, and we made it outside of Klayton's nice estate within fifteen minutes. There were gates surrounding his property and I wasn't sure how the hell we were going to get in.

"Look, I see Treasure's car. She is definitely here. Let's try calling her because there is no way around this damn gate," I pointed out. The gate had a wire at the top of it so any intruder that tried to climb over it would get electrocuted. The one thing I could say was I knew my daughter was safe while she was here.

"Let me climb this bitch like it's a raggedy hoe from the street. If I die then I die, but I want my sister to come home,," Luca argued and I knew he got his stubbornness from me.

"Luca, look at the top of the gate. The wire will fry your ass if you try it. Don't be stupid. Now get back in the car and let's call Treasure. That is all we can really do because his place is secured better than Fort Knox," I pointed out, and Luca reluctantly calmed down.

He grabbed his phone and started calling Treasure. Her phone rang three times and then it went to voicemail. "Fuck. Why isn't she answering the fucking phone?" Luca was visibly angry. He dialed her number again and left her a scathing message.

"All we can do is wait for her. Let's go back home and wait for her. She obviously isn't planning on coming home tonight and we can't make her." I was trying to be the voice of reason, especially knowing Luca still harbored some resentment for Klayton because of the past. Nothing good could come from sitting outside of Klayton's home especially with our car sticking out like a sore thumb.

"She knows damn well I don't want her fucking with no street nigga, especially Klayton Jackson. That nigga is still in the damn streets and she has a child she needs to think about. His lifestyle could put her and Genesis in danger," Luca complained. He finally put the key in the ignition and started driving away. "Is it really Klayton's lifestyle that you have an issue with, or is it the fact you still dislike Klayton from the past?" I asked.

"Pops, it's both. Hell, he couldn't keep that crazy bitch from killing AJ, so how do I know he would keep Treasure safe? Besides, if she ever gets married, she deserves better than a street nigga anyway. She needs to marry a square dude, like a doctor or a dentist. If you ask me, Treasure doesn't need to get married because we will always make sure she is good," Luca fussed.

"You can't handicap your sister, Luca. I know that you mean well, but she deserves to be happy. If it is meant for her to get married and have her own family one day, then she will. I understand you feel bad about not protecting her, and you are holding her back by holding on to that guilt," I tried explaining to Luca, but he was already appearing to shut down on me.

"Stop trying to psychoanalyze me, Pops. Treasure doesn't need to fall in love to be happy, and that is that."

# UNTITLED

**Luca**

Pops and I finally got back home, and it had been a stressful day. I was trying to keep up with my workload at my firm, make sure Jonah was good after shit went down between him and Brii, and now my sister was cavorting with the fucking enemy. I had no idea what the hell I would say to her when she finally made it home, but if I had to take away her car and drive her to and from school myself and lose out on making money, then I would do that. I didn't want her fucking with that nigga Klayton on any level, and I was going to make her feel me. Another reason I had been losing my mind was I found myself attracted to this woman that came in earlier trying to proposition on me on why she should be a partner in my law firm. Her name is Regina Gigi Reynolds, and she was a redhead that was stacked with curves in all of the right places. She is about five foot six, 185 pounds and had a Hershey milk chocolate complexion. She reminded me of that damn Kelis song "Milkshake' because her backside would bring all of the boys to the mothafuckin' yard. I shouldn't be attracted to any other woman knowing that the love of my life, AJ, was dead and never coming back.

"Luca, come have some tea with me in the kitchen," my mom ordered and I knew I had no choice. If it was up to me, I would chill in my man cave all day and blast SportsCenter the rest of the night with an ice cold beer. I got up to meet my mother in the kitchen, and she knew me better than anyone else.

"What's up, Mom? Are you ok? Treasure is safe. I would have brought her home but I had no way to get into Klayton's mansion," I tried reassuring my mother.

"Luca, I am worried about you. A mother always knows when there is something wrong with her child, and I really want you to reconsider going back to therapy."

"Did Pops say anything to you?" I asked.

"No, but remember you are my first born and I always know when something isn't right with one of my kids. I know that you still blame yourself for protecting Treasure, but everything happened how God wanted it to. We wouldn't have Genesis if things didn't happen the way they did," my mom reminded me.

"Mom, no disrespect, but fuck God. Where was God when Treasure was raped repeatedly? Where was he when Genesis was born blind due to an STD? Where was God when AJ died, and where was he when Shae stopped taking her medication for bipolar disorder? If God is so powerful, then why does he allow bad things to happen?" I cried, and my mom wrapped me in her arms.

We cried together and lost track of time, and I didn't realize Pops had joined us as well. He was hugging both of us, trying to keep us together.

"I can't apologize enough, son. I still see how broken you are from the past and I realize that I really screwed you up. I love you, Genesis and Treasure more than life itself, and it hurts me to see you hurting. I didn't realize how bad you were hurting until we talked in the car, and it is okay to get help, son. You are still grieving, which is fine, but what you are doing is not normal," Pops tried convincing me.

"Man, I haven't told anyone but I have been having nightmares about AJ's murder. They went away after a year, but now they are starting to come back and they are back more frequently,," Luca admitted.

"I am glad you said something, Luca, and we are going to make an appointment for you to see a psychiatrist. The PTSD symptoms are coming back, and your father and I want you to be happy. Please promise me you will go. Don't do it for me or your father. Do it for yourself. You owe it to yourself to get better for you so you can live a happy life. I love you, Luca," my mom whispered and I had tears in my eyes.

I tried to be strong all of the time, especially with Treasure in the household. I couldn't show any sign of weakness when I needed to protect her and make sure she was good. It was hard trying to be the strong one all of the time, and I was wearing down. Not to mention, I was getting more and more clients at my law firm, which meant less time for me to spend with my family. It was a blessing my business was thriving as good as it was, but I also was becoming overwhelmed with my workload. I was really considering bringing Regina on board with the possibility of making her a partner if things worked out, but I had to make sure to keep things strictly platonic between us. It was never a good idea to mix business and pleasure.

"I want to see if the nightmares go away on their own first. I know they have been getting worse, but they might go away on their own."

Truthfully, I was trying to convince myself of the truth. Deep down, I knew I needed help, but I thought I would be okay if I ignored the nightmares.

"Luca, we can't force you to get help but we also don't want to go back to New York worried about you and Treasure. Your mother and I want to be sure that you guys will good and if you guys need us to stay for a while, then we definitely can. You have more than enough room for us and I don't want to be across the country and something happens to one of you guys." My father looked worried, and I needed to reassure him that we would be okay.

"Treasure and I will be fine. I don't want you guys to disrupt your lives behind us. You know I will always look out for my sister," I tried reassuring them, and I wasn't sure if it was working.

"Family will always come first,, Luca and I don't care if we gotta move to Timbuktu to make sure you guys are good. Giovanni and I would do that in a second. I will go with you if you need that support to go back to therapy, but you really need to consider going," My mother begged.

I never wanted to see my mother upset over me and if this would get her off of my back and stop worrying about me, then I would consider it. "If it makes you guys happy, then I just might go."

# 11

## REGINA "GIGI" REYNOLDS

Let a real bih make an appearance in this story. I am sure Luca told you all about my fine ass, but I go by Gigi. My ass is a corporate attorney, and I win ninety-eight percent of my fucking cases. I am a Pitbull in the courtroom and a beast in a bedroom. The problem with me is I can't commit to these fraudulent, pussy ass niggas in these streets. Either their dick is too little or they come with bitch ass tendencies, and my ass is not beat for the bullshit. It will take a real ass nigga to get me to settle down and by the way, my panties were wet during my interview with Luca; he might just be that nigga. Honey, my panties were Niagara Falls wet when I shook his hands, and I felt butterflies in the pit of my stomach. Let me tell you, when it comes to men, my ass is picky. If his dick is too little, I can't fuck with him. I went out with one nigga once and salivated over his dick print, only to find out he stuffed that shit with Charmin toilet paper. Fraudulent ass nigga, and my ass is on the fuck these niggas kinda time. If his beard looks like it hasn't been cleaned in days, it's a hell no. If his jeans are tighter than mine, then my ass is calling my gay friend Jeremy and setting their asses up. I might act ghetto right now, but my demeanor is professional when I hit the courtroom. I'm a hood professional so don't get me twisted. I am professional in the workplace and ghetto as fuck off of the clock.

"Earth to Gigi. Bih, where are you at?" Candice smirked, and she had caught me deep in thought. We were at TGI Friday's ordering a round of drinks. Candice is my younger sister and my best friend. We tell each other everything in our lives, and I would give my life for her. Candice is twenty-five years old and I am twenty-nine. Both of our parents were murdered when I was fifteen and Candice was eleven. We were sent to live with our aunt after our parents died and she was heaven sent, but nothing ever replaces the love of your parents. Our aunt Elena died when Candice turned twenty-one and now, we were all we really had. Elena had two biological kids that resented us and never liked us when we moved in with them. I had always been on my grind to make sure my sister was good, and I would give my life for hers, no questions asked.

"I'm here. Where is Marina's black ass at? You should have told her ass to get here at three o'clock, then she would have made it here on time," I complained. Marina Martinez was my best friend that wasn't blood-related, and she was thirty-one years old. She is an attorney as well and I met her when I was hired at my old law firm. The only time she would be on time to anything was if she had to go to court.

"Girl, you know she probably still fighting her baby daddy's hoe, Serena. That bitch needs an ass whooping leaving her one-year-old child on their doorstep in the damn cold," Candice complained.

"You know she used that baby as a come-up baby. I love Marina, but she needs to beat that fuck nigga Anthony's ass because she wouldn't keep having these problems if she kept that nigga in check. Niggas like Anthony is why I hoe mothafuckas. There isn't a man out there that can keep his dick in his pants—"

"Excuse me, ma'am. I hate to interrupt your conversation, but I just wanted to say how beautiful you are ma'am. My name is

Darnell "Big Dick" Johnson, and my name speaks for itself. I can show you more than I can tell you," he bragged, and this nigga really grabbed his package in front of me. Candice started laughing her ass off because she knew I always attracted these batshit crazy ass niggas.

"Nigga, you got me fucked up hoe! You come over to my table looking like fucking Patrick from SpongeBob. I bet your ass is only working with a little baby carrot in your pants because your hand can't even grip your package right. Go get your shrimp dick ass away from my table before I stab your ass, you raggedy bitch" I fussed as I grabbed my pocket knife out of my purse.

"Fuck you, bougie ass bitch. Your pussy stank anyway—" Those were the last words he got out of his mouth before I cut his ass one good time with my knife. Candice got up and punched him in the face. I didn't even notice that Marina had arrived, and we started stomping this nigga out.

Security came and got in the middle of us and broke up the brawl, and "Big Dick Johnson" was on the floor covering his face up. Pussy ass bitch couldn't even try to take on the three of us. The restaurant manager came up to us apologizing.

"Your meal will be on the house, ladies. I saw this guy come up to your table disturbing you ladies. I apologize for the disturbance." The manager apologized, but the situation wasn't his fault.

"No worries. Just get this bastard away from this table. Thank you." I sat back down, and Marina and Candice sat down while security excused the nigga away.

"Where you been, bih? You been blowing Anthony's mic again?" I clowned Marina.

"Shut up, bih. That bitch Serena showed up claiming she pregnant with twins by Anthony and I beat her ass in the face. Anthony got mad at me for putting my hands on a pregnant woman. I cussed his black ass out and threw him out of the house again—"

"Bih, you know that nigga will be back home within two days. I don't know why you put up with that community dick ass nigga," I fussed and flagged the waiter over so I could order another round of drinks. Shit like this was why I believed in the motto *niggas ain't shit*. I fuck 'em and send 'em packing because all they are good for is a good nut.

"Anthony is all I know and I love him. I am getting sick of his shit. I am tempted to make a pitcher of Kool-Aid using Fabuloso and poison his ass." Marina had tears in her eyes and I could tell she was getting fed up. "You are way too good for that nigga. Fuck history, Marina. Anthony isn't treating you the way that you deserve to be treated. You know we will be here for you when you are ready to leave his ass alone for good," Candice replied. We changed the subject and enjoyed the rest of our girls night out without any more drama.

# TREASURE

I woke up the next morning in an unfamiliar surroundings, and I almost panicked. All of my clothes were still on so I knew I hadn't been violated, but I didn't recognize the room I was in. I smelled food coming from the kitchen and then I remembered that I was still at Klayton's house. Luca and my dad were going to fucking kill me because I never came home yesterday after that argument with my parents. I didn't bother to jump in the shower and I went downstairs to see Klayton making a couple of plates. He had went to IHOP and got takeout. I prayed he got breakfast and not that nasty ass lunch shit that they serve.

"You were knocked out like a light, Treasure. I went to get some food since I can't cook for shit. I got some pancakes and bacon from IHOP. I hope you like that." Klayton smiled and I could feel my heart pounding in my chest.

"That smells delicious and yes, I will take a plate." My stomach was growling and I sat down at the table. He passed me my plate and a glass of orange juice.

I know we lost track of time last night, but nothing happened between us. I wanted you to be comfortable so I put you in the guest room, and I hope you were comfortable."

"Thank you, Klayton. You are such a gentleman. I need to leave after I finish eating because I am sure my parents and Luca have to be worried by now."

"Word. I am going to follow you and make sure you get home safely, and I am not taking no for an answer," Klayton insisted.

"Klayton, if Luca sees you—"

"I don't fear no nigga so if he is with the shits and he wants it, he can get it. Treasure, I plan to show and prove that I am in this with you for the long run. I need to go pick my daughter up so I will follow you home and then go pick her up," Klayton explained, and I could tell there was no changing his mind.

"Fine, Klayton. What are you going to dress Danielle up as for Halloween? Genesis wants to be a princess and I want to take her trick or treating. I know it is harder because of her eyesight, but I want her to have as normal of a childhood as possible," I explained and Klayton's eyes softened.

"Danielle wants to be a bumblebee. I still need to go get her costume. She is super excited for Halloween. We should make it a date and take the kids trick or treating together."

"Do you think it is a good idea considering we are so new? I don't want to bring random men around my daughter—"

"I am not no random nigga, my name is Klayton Jackson and put some mothafucking respeck on my name. We would be on an even playing field because I don't bring women around my daughter. Have you taken Genesis trick or treating before?" Klayton asked.

"No, but my parents always take her in New York and I want her to live as normal of a life as possible. If anyone makes fun of my daughter because of her disability, then I will beat their ass, straight up—"

"Treasure, you are a queen and you don't have to lower yourself to the level of a peasant. If anyone gets out of pocket while we take the kids trick or treating, I will handle it. You don't even have to worry because no one will try you guys when you guys are with me. A real nigga like myself always stays strapped," Klayton bragged. I felt safe around him and I knew he would make sure Genesis and I were good.

"Are you sure? I mean—"

"I never say anything that I don't mean, Treasure. Hell, we can go trick or treating early and bring the girls back here to play together. Are there any special toys she likes playing with? I will make sure to load up on whatever Genesis needs to feel comfortable," Klayton promised.

"Yeah, I can put a list together for you. I am touched because I never met a man like you," I admitted and got up to throw our paper plates away.

"I used to be really reckless and I am far from perfect, but when I love someone, I love hard, Treasure. I know that woman is going to be you ,so you better get used to my mansion." Klayton smiled.

"You mean your damn fort, Klayton. No one could get in here even if they tried."

"I have to because of the lifestyle that I live. I will spare no cost to make sure the ones that I love are safe at all costs and by any means necessary. Go ahead and get dressed so I can take you home, though." Klayton licked his lips and I was turned on by the sight of this sexy beast.

It was weird because I couldn't remember the last time I felt aroused by a man. I assumed that I would never have a healthy relationship with another man because of my past. I walked closer to Klayton, stepped on my tiptoes and wrapped my arms around his neck. This nigga was truly like a big teddy bear, and I couldn't get enough of him. He picked me up and I wrapped my legs around him. I kissed him passionately on the lips and surprised both of us. My tongue slipped inside his mouth and I was gone. We made out for a few minutes, and I could feel him rubbing on my breasts. I was so turned, on he could have his way with me on the kitchen counter if he wanted to, but he broke the kiss and put me down.

"Treasure, you doing too much to a nigga. If you didn't know it before, your ass is mine now. If you don't want any fucking bodies on your hands, then you know not to even look at another nigga, on god."

# 12

# LUCA

I woke up and the first thing I did was go to see if Treasure came home, and I was pissed off to see that she hadn't been home. Her bed was still disheveled the way it was last night, and the thought of my sister fucking had me big ass mad. I couldn't wait for my sister to come home and give her a piece of my mind. The only thing saving her right now was the fact I had to go to work. I had a dream about Gigi last night and tossed and turned in my sleep. I kept imagining myself slipping my tongue in between her wet folds and woke up having to relieve myself, if you get my drift, this morning. I finished my business and went to check on my niece, Genesis, and she was sleeping comfortably. I kissed her on the cheek and then went to make myself some breakfast. I was pleasantly surprised to see my mother in the kitchen cooking some fried potatoes, grits and toast.

"Luca, breakfast is almost ready. Come have a seat. I want to be sure you go to work on a full stomach," my mom insisted. She didn't have to tell me twice and I was ready to dig in. My mom made me a plate, and my father came into the kitchen.

"How are you feeling this morning, Luca?" My father looked concerned and I didn't want them to worry about me.

"I am good. Just tired as I didn't sleep well. I'm getting Trea-sure's ass when she does come home—"

I was interrupted by the sound of the front door opening and I jumped out of my seat. I heard my sister talking to someone in a hushed whisper and I saw red. I knew she was talking to that nigga Klayton, and I was about to give them both a piece of my mind. I hurried toward the front door and grabbed my sister by her neck.

"Luca, what the hell?" Treasure cried and she looked terrified. She started crying and I instantly felt bad for my actions. I didn't mean to grab her the way that I did, but I lost it once I knew she had arrived with that nigga at my house.

I didn't even get to respond before I felt a punch to my face. Klayton and I started going rounds again, and this nigga had heart going to war over my sister. I tried pinning Klayton's big ass down but his size was too much for me, although I was matching him blow for blow. Treasure was crying in the background and I vowed to make things right with her later. I needed to show this nigga that he needed to leave my sister alone. My father finally got in the middle and broke up the fight, although I kept trying to get out of my father's grip.

"Klayton, bring your black ass back here for another round of this ass whooping! You want it, come get it homie. You violating smashing my sister and shit, man!" I yelled at the top of my lungs.

"I didn't have sex with Treasure. Nigga, I don't need to lie on my fucking dick. Now, I'm gonna tell you one good time to keep your hands off Treasure. If you are mad at anyone then be mad at me, but what you are not going to do is put your hands on my future wife and think shit is sweet. Next time, I will put a bullet in the dome; try that, nigga," Klayton spat and he showed no fear. I almost spazzed out when he called Treasure his future wife.

"Fuck you. Over my dead body will Treasure marry a fucking thug like you that has fucked all of the single women in the Los Angeles area. She deserves better than a nigga in the streets, and

I will protect her from herself if I have to," I spat, and Klayton's face was red.

"Luca you are a fucking hypocrite. Your ass used to be in the streets the same way Klayton is with Jonah, yet you are judging him because of your past issues with him. I am sick of you trying to run my life and dictate what I can or can't do. I feel like I am living in prison. If I want to be with Klayton, then you will not stop me!" Treasure screamed.

"Everyone, enough yelling and screaming! Klayton, Treasure is good and she will call you later. This is a family matter we are dealing with." My father dismissed him, yet he wasn't moving. He really did not give any fucks.

"Treasure, are you okay?" Klayton asked. I could tell he really had feelings for my sister and he cared about her, but she deserved better than what Klayton had to offer her.

"Klayton, go ahead and go. I will call you later." Treasure blew a kiss at him and I almost lost it again, but my father pushed my ass back into the house. Klayton finally left and I stood there staring at my sister, who was looking at me defiantly. If looks could kill, she would have died and been resurrected, only for me to kill her ass again.

"Treasure, what the fuck are you doing with that man? You realize all you are to him is another hoe, right?" I asked although deep down, I knew I was wrong. I knew the look of a man in love, and Klayton was in love with my sister. I was going to deny that shit and find a way to keep them apart. My sister was gullible and naïve, and it was times like this I had to step in and do what was best for her. She would thank me for this later, even if I was the villain now.

"I don't owe you an explanation, Luca. I was at Klayton's house last night and we spent all night talking. We lost track of time and I ended up staying the night. Nothing sexual happened between us—"

"And nothing ever will, sis. You might think I am the bad guy but I really am trying to protect you. I know what is best for you. I love you more than life itself, and it is my job to protect you from yourself. I apologize for putting my hands on you but seeing you with that nigga pissed me off. You are beautiful, smart and caring, and you don't need a man for anything. I will always make sure you are good financially so you never have to depend on another man for shit. You have family that loves and cares for you. What do you need to date for?" I asked.

"Luca, I love you. I know that was in the moment, so I am not even going to hold your lack of judgment against you. You need to let me live my life and find my happiness. I know that you want me to be happy, but you want it by your definition of what should make me happy. That is unfair to me. I cannot continue living life in a box because that allows you to feel comfortable," Treasure pleaded.

Our father stepped in and intervened. "Luca, I know you want what is best for Treasure and I know she loves you. I can even understand you feeling betrayed because of your past with Klayton, but he loves my daughter. I could see in his eyes he is in love with her. If you keep trying to keep them from being together, you will only end up pushing them together and Treasure will end up hating you," my father explained. I didn't understand why my father was ok with Treasure dating Klayton.

I refused to hear what he was saying because I was not able to come to terms with my sister moving forward with her life, especially with that nigga. I didn't want her dating anyone, but why did it have to be Klayton out of all people?

"Out of all niggas, why would my sister fuck with a man that had sex with my dead ex-girlfriend? Where is the loyalty, sis? You know that nigga is gonna cheat on you the same way he did all of his past hoes."

"Get over it, Luca. That shit with AJ happened more than three years ago, and Klayton owed you no fucking loyalty. Your issue was with AJ and deep down, you know you still blame

Klayton for AJ's death even though we all know that wasn't his fault. You are looking to place blame where there isn't anyone other than Shae to blame for that bullshit. I love you, Luca, more than life itself, but you cannot continue forcing me to live in a box because that is what you want." Treasure was crying and it broke my heart to see my little sister crying.

"I will never get over AJ's death. I will always blame Klayton for not controlling his hoes and if you love me like you say you do, then you will make the right choice. I am going to give you some time and space to think about it, Treasure, and I hope you make the right decision."

# BRII

The night that doctor bitch called Jonah, he tried pleading his case and begging for my forgiveness, but I had no words for him. I kicked his ass out of the house and he had been staying in a hotel until I decided to let him come home. I loved my husband with everything in me, but what he did was wrong. He claimed he was only taking her out to get pictures to use for evidence to report to the state, but do I look that stupid? We had just had a fight at the hospital and I am supposed to believe he didn't give the doctor his number out of spite because he was pissed off at me? I knew I wrong for popping off the way that I did at the hospital, but Joseline Becker knew what the fuck she was doing. Nikki and Kobe Jackson came over and took the kids off my hands and Jonah had my ass banned from visiting Leslie in the hospital, claiming he didn't want any more problems between me and the doctor bitch.

"Hey bitch, get your ass up. We are going to go out and stunt on these niggas." Rolonda walked right into my house as if she owned it. She was wearing a red strapless dress that highlighted all of her curves, topped off with a pair of Versace heels. Ro was looking delicious and if I was into girls, I would be tempted to eat her snatch, but I wasn't.

"Go away, Ro. I don't feel like going out. You know damn well Trayce will drag your ass out of the club" I reminded her.

"Girl, ain't no one stunting Trayce's crazy ass. You need to get out of the house, looking like Mrs. Doubtfire, Brii. I brought over a couple outfits that would look great on your figure, so I need you to chop chop and get dressed. You don't have a say in this, so you better hurry up and get ready." Ro smiled. I appreciate her, but the last thing I felt like doing was going to the club and having to shoot down thirsty ass niggas.

"I rather stay home and drink my bottle of wine-"

"No more feeling sorry for yourself, Brii. We are going to get you out of this funk and if Jonah doesn't appreciate you, the next nigga will so get up and get ready," Ro ordered.

"Rolonda, you know I am a married woman and—"

"Shit, you were married when he gave that doctor whore his number and he knew what he was doing then, so turnabout is fair play. Brii, I am not saying you need to cheat on your husband, but a little revenge is in order. Men can never take the bullshit that they dish out, and it is time for you to entertain another nigga—"

"Are you trying to get me fucking killed? That sounds like some crazy shit that can backfire on us. I am having enough marital issues already, Ro. This doesn't sound like a good idea." As mad as I was at Jonah, I didn't know if I had the heart to dish out the same treatment that he gave me. Granted I had a secret that I was keeping from Jonah but that was something he would never find out.

"Brii, these niggas will never learn until you show them that you are not to be fucked with. Yes, you were wrong for how you handled the situation, but Jonah should have checked that bitch on sight and made it known that he wouldn't tolerate his wife being disrespected. You aren't going to fuck the new guy, but we are going to teach Jonah that you have options out here," Ro preached. I was slowly starting to warm up to the idea, although part of me thought something would go wrong.

"Listen, Ro, if shit hits the fan, I am blaming you for this fucked up ass idea. What outfits did you have picked out for me?" I asked eagerly. I could use a night out to get back to myself because lately, I haven't been feeling like myself.

"Girl, I found this blue dress that flatters your curves and the last pair of Ferragamo heels. I had to cop us both a pair, although I am not wearing mine tonight. Go take a shower and when you get out, I am going to do your hair. We are going to stunt on some hoes tonight!" Ro started twerking, and that cheered me up a bit.

"Jonah is going to regret entertaining that damn doctor, and we are going to have a good time tonight. I will not sulk over a nigga that is probably out there living his best life." I started walking toward my bathroom.

"Girl, that is the fucking spirit. And I have my mace and a gun if these niggas want to get out of pocket tonight, so you will be safe. You won't end up doing anything you regret because we are going in together and we are leaving together."

# 13

## JONAH

I went to visit Leslie earlier and luckily, it looked like he would be able to come home tomorrow if all continued to go well. His leg was in a cast and he hadn't had any symptoms of a concussion, so I felt like I dodged a bullet. I decided to bring Les with me to the hotel until Brii and I settled our differences.

My phone rang and I saw Luca was calling me, so I answered.

"What's up, bruh?"

"Yo, shit hitting the fan, but I will tell you about that later. I got in a fight with Treasure this morning and went to work to get my mind off things. I didn't feel like going home after work so I decided to hit this little spot called Breeze up, and you won't believe who I see in there partying like her hoe ass ain't married." Luca spat. I was curious as to who he saw in the club but as long as it wasn't Brii out there acting like a slut, it didn't matter to me.

"Man, what happened with you and Treasure? You know I am not tripping on no bird shit." I wasn't the type of nigga to partake in gossip and Luca wasn't either, which is why I was surprised about this conversation.

"Man, Brii and Ro are in the club dropping it like it's hot, and I saw sis entertaining niggas. What the hell did you do to piss little sis off?" Luca asked and I saw red. I grabbed the purple vase that was on the table in my hotel room and threw it against the wall. It shattered into tiny little pieces and I knew I would be getting a nice little bill for the damage.

"Man, that doctor bitch called my phone while I was dicking Brii down and Brii answered the phone. Now, she mad because she thinks a nigga has been cheating on her and shit. She kicked me out the house and calls herself not fucking with mem and now she out there being a fucking bird. I think the fuck not. Are you still at Breeze?" I asked Luca.

"Hell yeah, nigga. I hid where Ro and Brii can't see me but I can still keep my eyes on them. If they leave, I'ma follow them and shoot you a text. Hurry up and get here, man." Luca was looking out for me, even when it was clear that he was going through something. This nigga was my brother and I would always make sure he was good.

"Thanks for looking out, bro. I am getting dressed and will be on my way in a few minutes." I hung up the phone and started counting to ten in my head. I had to calm myself down so I would make it to Breeze in one piece and drag Brii's ass back home kicking and screaming.

I got in the car and made it to the club in less than fifteen minutes. I texted Luca, and he told me that Brii was still in the club partying it up. I made it inside and found Luca with a table in the corner and bottle service going. I gave his ass dap.

"What up, bruh? Where did you see the two thots at?" I asked, not caring that I was being disrespectful. When they said that men can't take the disrespectful shit that they dish out, it is so true. Now, the roles were reversed and I didn't like being in Brii's position one bit. Now, I knew how she felt when that whore was in my face blatantly flirting with me and I should have checked her ass. I had never cheated on Brii, but I left room for Brii to become insecure by not checking the bitch immediately.

"Man, she is over there." Luca pointed out and I saw red. Brii was near the bar talking to this flaming orange tickle me Elmo faggot ass nigga, and she was about to have a body on her fucking hands tonight. I didn't say anything else before I grabbed my piece from my pocket and strode over in their direction.

Ro must have tapped Brii on her shoulder and warned her because I saw Brii look in my direction with a look of fear on her face. She better get scared because Zaddy was about to tap that ass tonight.

I didn't even bother addressing Brii right away. I turned my head to the flaming hot Cheetos-looking nigga and starting talking shit. "Nigga, who the fuck are you talking to my damn wife? Your ass violating coming for what is mine."

The nigga really started flailing his arms in the air like a little pussy. "I'm sorry, let me go and I will never bother you again—"

"You are a fucking pussy. Your ass trying to talk to my wife yet you can't even protect her, GI Joe." I smirked. I grabbed my gun and pistol-whipped him with it, and blood spewed everywhere. Brii started screaming while Ro looked amused. I forgot her ass was crazy and with the shits too.

"My name is Jarrett, not GI Joe," he cried, and Luca was dying laughing at this nigga.

"Brii, you would choose to fuck with a pussy ass nigga," Luca fussed. Brii rolled her eyes and had an attitude on her face. As far as I was concerned, she had no real reason to be mad.

"I said your name is GI Joe, so that's what it is. Now, take your fake fuck it in the booty ass and get the fuck outta here before I shoot your ass." I threatened and it looked like GI Joe was fading in and out of consciousness.

"How can I leave when I can barely see? My vision is blurred." GI Joe started foaming at the mouth and his body started shaking like he was having a seizure.

"Oh shit. We gotta get out of here!" Luca grabbed Ro and threw her over his shoulder bridal style while I picked Brii up.

"Put me down, asshole. I need to call 911 so he can get medical attention before he dies—"

I didn't even let Brii finish her statement before I pulled my gun out and put two bullets in the dome, instantly killing the man. I didn't need his ass snitching to the police on some bull-shit, so his time on earth came to an end.

"Luca, text Klayton to send his crew to clean up this body," I fussed as we ran out of the club. It was a struggle because Brii was hitting my back, trying to get me to put her down.

"Done, nigga. Go get Brii settled and I will holla at you when I get Ro back to her husband," Luca replied, and we went our separate ways.

Shooting that nigga in the club wasn't exactly the smartest thing to do but hopefully, Klayton came through and helped a nigga out.

"Why did you have to shoot that man? He did nothing to you and you might end up going to jail for murder? Our kids need you, Jonah, and we left that lifestyle alone three years ago," Brii complained like a petulant two-year-old. I threw her ass in the car and went and got in on the driver's side. I pulled away like a bat out of hell and ignored Brii for the moment as I wasn't stunting her bullshit. I called Klayton, just to make sure Luca followed through because I knew Luca still harbored ill feelings toward him. I couldn't afford to get caught slipping with that body left in the club.

"Yo Jonah, I got the text from Luca which threw me off guard because we recently got in a fight. Of course, I got your back. My crew is already there handling the body and as soon as it is handled, they are sending me proof. I also have them getting the video from the club so there is no proof anything happened," Klayton explained.

"Thank you for looking out, man. What the hell you mean you and Luca got in a fight?" I asked curiously. Even Brii sat up in her seat ear hustling because she wanted to know what was up.

"I am surprised Luca didn't tell you, but it isn't my place to tell. I will holla at you as soon as I get the picture and forward that to you so you know the body was handled," Klayton answered abruptly before he hung up. Klayton was a real nigga, especially doing me a favor that he didn't have to do.

I pulled up to the house and then it hit me: where the hell were Antoinette and Blake while Brii was out thotting?

"Where in the hell is Antoinette and Blake at while you out there doing you?" I demanded and I was pissed off again at Brii for putting me in this situation.

"Nigga please, I don't owe you any fucking explanation!" Brii yelled and slammed my car door. I quickly caught up to Brii walking to the front door and pressed her body against the front door.

"You know I don't want the neighbors in our business, but I will take it there if you don't give me the answers I am looking for." I snapped and Brii spit in my face. I blacked out at that point and backhanded her one good time.

*Whap! Whap!*

"Nigga, you really put your hands on me?" Brii looked shocked, and I immediately felt bad. I never would have put my hands on her, and I knew our marriage was really in a bad spot.

"Brii, I am sorry. I didn't mean to hit you and I blacked out—"

"Jonah, get your ass away from me before I call the cops on your ass for assault," Brii whispered. She was a little too calm for my liking, which meant she was about to go the fuck off on my ass.

"Word, Brii? You know how I feel about the fucking police. You got that, and you know you were foul for spitting in my damn face. Maybe we should get a divorce!" I yelled angrily.

"Nigga, you are not going to keep throwing divorce in my face every time we have a fight, Jonah. If you want a divorce, you can have it. Come back in a few days and get your shit out of this house!" Brii walked in the door and slammed the door in my face.

That conversation certainly went left, and I was hoping to check Brii about her behavior at the club. Instead, it looked like I was headed toward a divorce and I didn't know what to do anymore. The logical thing should have been to go take my ass back to the hotel and think things over. Why did I end up calling the good ole doctor to see if she was available for a late night date?

# GIGI

I am of the motto that time waits for no one. I decided to pop back up at Luca's firm to see if he thought about my offer to become part of the team. I am confident in the skill set that I have and know that I would be an added asset to the team and it would be his loss if he didn't accept my offer.

"Hello is Mr. Glover here?" I asked politely and the receptionist Brianna rolled her eyes at me. She was lucky that I really wanted this opportunity because I would have dragged her ass across the room and asked questions later.

"Do you have an appointment? If not, I am afraid you will have to reschedule." Brianna smiled. I knew this bitch wanted to fuck Luca and part of me wondered why I even gave a shit. Luca is a good looking man but he is like all niggas. They ain't shit. I never shit where I eat so I would never fuck someone that I was working with so that would be a second strike working against Luca.

I counted to ten in my head before I responded. "Listen here, Miss Piggy. I do not have an appointment and—"

I was interrupted by the front door opening and Luca Glover's big ass himself walked in the office. His appearance was a bit disheveled but the imperfection even looked good on him. He had bags under his eyes like he hadn't slept in a couple of days and something in me wanted to comfort him.

"Ms. Reynolds I am surprised to see you. Give me just a couple of minutes to get some coffee and you can come back to see me." Luca greeted me with a warm smile.

"Mr. Glover she doesn't have an appointment and should follow protocol—"

"Brianna I got this thank you. Besides my eleven o'clock appointment sent me a text saying they needed to reschedule so I am free." Luca checked her ass and my panties were soaked. Normally I am not into light-skinned men but Luca's ass could fucking get it.

Brianna looked like she wanted to protest but she knew better than to challenge Luca. "My apologies Luca. You know I just wanted to look out for you," she cooed.

Luca didn't respond to her but gestured to me to follow him into his office so I did. "Would you like something to drink? I have water, juice, tea or coffee."

"No thank you. From one lawyer to another you have a future sexual harassment lawsuit in your future if you don't do something about your receptionist. She was very rude when I came in here looking for you."

Luca nodded his head before he poured himself a cup of coffee. "I am very sensitive about that because of a past situation in the workplace. I am trying to handle Brianna with a long-handed spoon but I have been documenting everything in the event that I have to terminate her. What brings you in to see me today?" Luca asked quickly getting down to business.

"I just wanted to check in and see if you thought about the offer I presented you with the last time I came in. I know the value that I would bring to your law firm and you have had a huge increase in clientele so I know you can use another set of hands on your staff. I am hardworking and my success rate at my previous law firm speaks for itself. I have a ninety-eight percent success rate with cases so that speaks for itself." I was tooting my own horn a bit but I deserved to. If I didn't go hard for myself then who will? Working with Luca Glover is an opportunity that was a once in a lifetime opportunity because he has built up a big-time name in the field in the three years that he owned his own firm. I could see myself doing big things in the future with his law firm. I just needed the opportunity to make shit shake.

"I know we didn't have much time to talk the last time but I wanted to know why you left your last law firm. I saw on your resume that you worked at Schumer Law and Company for two years after you passed your bar exam. Why did you end up leaving?" Luca asked and he stared straight at me. He was giving me butterflies in the pit of my stomach which was a feeling I was unused to feeling. The only time I had any sort of romantic feelings was for my ex-fiancé named James. We met in law school and went from a quick fling to falling in love. He proposed six months after we started dating and everything went well until I caught him having sex with his male best friend. I not only dumped his ass but took a picture of him being a booty bandit and spread it all over the school campus. James was so humiliated that he ended up dropping out and transferring to another law school and I haven't seen him since. I went and got a check up to make sure he didn't give me any STDs or diseases that I would have to live with for the rest of my life and learned the lesson that niggas ain't shit.

"Are you ok? You spaced out on me for a second." Luca looked concerned. I was embarrassed because I was attracted to a man I had no business being attracted to.

"I'm good. Sorry about that. Schumer Law was great to me for my first two years after graduating. I wanted a chance to move up and advance in the company and that opportunity just was not going to happen there. I am a young educated African-American woman and I was putting in major work for the company but not getting compensated adequately. When I first started, I knew that I was going to have to prove myself and show that I deserved a seat at the table with the big boys. What worked against me is being a female and being African-American because I overheard them saying they really hired me so I would be their token African-American so they couldn't be accused of discrimination. The straw that broke the camel's back was a year and a half after I was hired they promoted a white guy that had only started six months before me and he was lower on the totem pole. I realized that I would never be appreciated there and took a leap of faith and quit recently." I admitted.

"I must say I admire your drive and your determination Regina. Being a minority myself I can understand and empathize with your dilemma. Your resume is also impeccable and speaks for itself. I had a background check ran on you and everything you are telling me has checked out. Obviously, I am not looking for a partner right now, but I would not mind hiring you on a trial basis as an associate to start. If everything works out then I will definitely have an opportunity open for a partner in the future if you are open to that. I will put that in your employment contract that you will have a fair opportunity as a partner so you know I am not fucking you over excuse my language. How does that sound?" Luca asked.

I was impressed by his professional demeanor and I could tell he legitimately was trying to give me a fair and reasonable chance. "That sounds good and well but you know I am going to ask you how much I am going to be making."

Luca and I both let out a laugh before he answered. " Since you have experience I will start you out at $150,000 with incentives and performance bonuses included. You will have sick leave, vacation leave, and paternity leave if needed. If you agree to take this position, you will see that I am a very fair man and I will not take advantage of you. I understand that you need time to think it over. Here is my business phone and my personal cell phone number if you need anything." Luca held his hand out for a handshake and I eagerly accepted. It seemed like he held on to my hand for a long period of time when in reality it was only a few seconds.

"Um thank you, Mr. Glover. I will let you know. I just need a few days to think about it and I will get back to you...

## 14

## KLAYTON

"Yo let me get a bottle of Henny," I ordered. The lady behind the counter at the liquor store went to retrieve the bottle when a little boy ran smack dab into my chest.

"My bad nigga!" He yelled and he puffed his little chest out like he was doing something. Whoever little kid this was had some mothafucking balls and I liked him already.

I crouched down to get down to his level. " What's up little man? My name is Klayton. What is your name?"

"My name is Little Jah!" Jah smiled. I could tell this kid is bad as fuck but where the fuck was his parents at? There was something about this little boy that reminded me of myself although I didn't have this much heart when I was his age.

"Jahquel get your ass back here. I'm whoop your ass when we get home!" This skinny blasian chick yelled and she finally walked up and grabbed his hand. She was kind of cute but I only have eyes for Treasure otherwise I would have been shooting my shot with this woman.

"Mya I want some Doritos!" Jah yelled as if he was the man of the house. This little nigga really was doing something and if I ever had a son he probably would act just like little Jah.

The lady named Mya turned to address me but the cashier interrupted us. "Is that all—?"

"Listen you little cock a doodle doo no weave having bucktooth ass hoe, you saw I was having a conversation right?" I hated when ignorant bitches interrupted a conversation and ignorant Klayton was coming out to play.

The cashier looked as if she was about to cry. "But you are holding up the line sir—"

I turned to address the line behind me. " Does it look like I give a fuck about people having to wait in line? They should have got here before we did so they can put the shit back or wait their turn. Do any of you butterfinger Michelin man looking bitches have any problems waiting a few minutes while—"

"Listen, nigga, I don't have time to listen to you kee kee on some bullshit—"

Before he could finish his sentence I pulled out my Glock and busted his ass between the eyes and his body fell to the ground. "Fuck you doing in the hood with your ole forty-five grab 'em by the pussy ass? I bet your ass not gonna talk that shit from the fucking dead," I spat. You can take a nigga out of the hood but you can never take the hood out of the nigga.

"Bang bang, nigga. Klayton went bang bang, nigga!" Little Jah yelled. He was jumping around with his fingers pointed in a shooting motion like he was about to set it off in this bitch. This little boy was a carbon copy of me except we didn't share any blood.

Mya stared at me like I lost my mind and I could tell she wanted to address Jah's behavior but she was shocked at the turn of events. "Let me pay for y'all stuff. I am sure you have a man at home so I'm not on no funny shit but my name is Klayton Jackson and—"

"The legend is fucking real. I thought you were just some character Thea's petty ass made up. Can I twerk for a real nigga?" Mya whispered.

"Naw I am real baby. I don't think that would be a good idea because I would hate to have to murk your nigga for coming at me over your pretty ass and I got a woman I plan on wifing up soon. Her name is Treasure and baby girl you pretty but you have nothing on Treasure. And this little boy you got over here—"

"My ass not little. My name is little Jah but ain't nothing little about me including my dick—"

Mya slapped Little Jah in the face. "Where did you learn to talk like that?"

"This little hoe Stephanie told me my pee pee is different from hers and she showed me at school. I showed her my pee pee and she said it's big," Little Jah whispered. Mya looked disgusted and embarrassed. She was shocked speechless. I was stunned and this little boy is bad as hell. This little boy was a player at the age of nine years old and shit I needed to school him before he got some little thot pregnant by the age of thirteen.

"Yo what school you go to Jah? Man let me tell you about these little hoes. Always wrap it up and don't bust in 'em raw. Remember what uncle Klayton told you when you get older. Promise little man?" I asked as I gave him dap.

"Yeah, and when I grow up I want to go bang bang like you did to that man."

"Jahquel, you are on punishment. I am taking your iPad and all your toys for a week until you learn how to act. Apologize to Klayton so we can go home," Mya lectured Jah and he smiled.

"Man you a real nigga Klayton and I want to be like you when I grow up." Little Jah gave my ass dap.

"Listen, man, you are gonna be a pre-teen soon and you gotta learn to be good for Mya. If you promise me to be good you can come trick or treating with me and my daughter. My girl Treasure has a four-year-old daughter named Genesis that will be coming with us." I explained and Jahquel looked excited. At first, I thought he was going to roll his eyes at the thought of trick or treating because he acts way too grown for his age.

"Listen I am not sure it is a good idea—" Mya started but Jah interrupted her.

"Please let me go trick or treating with Klayton. I will be a good little nigga I promise," Little Jah begged.

"Jah will be safe with me. I know you don't know me really well but I would love to chop it up with you and your man. It would be my honor to have Jah come with us." I wanted to reassure her that Jah would be safe because I understood how it was to trust your child with a stranger.

"I will need to talk to Derek about this first but how about I get your number and I can give you a call?" Mya suggested.

"Hell yeah let's swap digits." I grabbed my iPhone and gave it to her so she could put her phone number in it and she called my number from her phone. Once my number came up on her caller id she hung up and stored it in her contact information.

"I have a better idea Klayton. How about we make trick or treating an adventure? Derek and I will bring Jahquel and Davion and you and Treasure will have Genesis and your daughter and we can make a night of it. Wait a minute. Instead of trick or treating, maybe we could do a Halloween-themed party for the kids and we can buy the candy and hang out with them," Mya suggested.

Honestly, it wasn't a bad idea. It might be more fun and I am sure we could incorporate some games that Genesis could play due to her disability. "The only thing is Genesis is fully blind so we would need to have some activities that she could participate in but I am all for it."

"I am sorry. I didn't know she has a disability but we will definitely make sure we do activities she can participate in. Maybe we can sing Halloween songs and stuff karaoke style and have cookies and punch." Mya suggested.

"Just hit me up and we can talk about it, Mya. I gotta get going. Little Jah it was nice meeting you..."

# TREASURE

I was sitting in class barely paying attention because of the ultimatum Luca gave me. I couldn't believe he gave me an ultimatum to pick between him and Klayton. Was I being disloyal to my brother by wanting to explore things with Klayton? I felt like I was stuck in between a rock and a hard place because I really wanted to explore things with Klayton, but Luca wasn't having that at all.

"Class is dismissed. Make sure to have your outline ready for your class project ready by the next class session." My professor dismissed us and I eagerly jumped out of my chair. I was more than ready to go home for the day and play with my daughter.

I was so distracted I didn't notice Darnell's snake ass was following me until it was too late. "Treasure let me talk to you."

He blocked the path to my car so I couldn't enter my car. "Treasure, I just want to talk to you." This fool was almost Keith Sweat dry begging.

"We have nothing to talk about Darnell. Have you been using coke? You look a little psychotic." I tried pushing Darnell out of the way but he wasn't having it. His eyes looked like he was about to have a psychotic breakdown.

"Bitch do you think you are better than me? I am going to teach you a lesson that you will never forget," Darnell whispered and he pressed his body against mine. He forcefully stuck his tongue down my throat and my fight or flight instincts kicked in. I bit his tongue and then kicked him in the groin area and he fell to the ground crying.

I was disheveled trying to find my car keys so I could get in my car and try to run when I felt him grab my hair and pull my ass down to the ground. I almost hit my head on the concrete and I was praying I would find a way out of this situation. It was like déjà vu all over again going back to when Blach used to force himself on me.

"Please don't do this Darnell. We can talk about whatever you want to talk about just don't rape me!" I cried and I felt myself starting to break down again. I wouldn't survive if another man ended up violating me.

The next thing you know I heard the sound of a gun click and a gun was being pointed in Darnell's direction. "Nigga let her go!" The sound of Klayton's voice was music to my fucking ears. I had no idea how he knew I was in trouble but I was grateful he showed up in the nick of time. If Darnell managed to rape me, I don't know if I ever would have recovered from that.

"Oh shit Klayton this isn't what it looks like—" Darnell tried to plead. Klayton picked Darnell up from the ground and threw him in the trunk of his car. He ran to my side as I laid on the ground in a state of shock over what almost happened to me. There was no doubt in my mind that Darnell was going to rape me and he would have gotten away with it if Klayton hadn't shown up.

"Treasure come with me. I promise I will protect you and make sure you are ok. Did he hurt you?" Klayton asked while cradling my small body in his arms.

"He almost raped me like Blach did." I whimpered and tears slid down my cheek.

"Baby girl I promise you that nigga Darnell is going to die and I am going to take his life myself. I know I am asking a lot out of you right now but I need you to stay strong for me. Can you do that for me Treasure?" Klayton lifted my face to meet his and I looked directly into the eyes of my Superman. If I hadn't already known that I had feelings for him, this situation confirmed for me that Klayton was the one for me.

" I don't want to go home. I can't deal with my family right now. Can you take me to your house?" I asked. Part of me knew this was asking a lot out of him since he probably didn't want to have a strange woman around his daughter like that.

"I gotchu bae. You can stay with me as long as you like. I don't want you to have to worry about anything. I need to get your ass out of here and take Darnell's sorry ass to the warehouse…"

# 15

# BRII

I love Jonah with everything in me but our marriage was in serious trouble. We came too far to let our marriage go down the drain so I was looking up some marriage therapists in Los Angeles and was contemplating making an appointment. The only thing stopping me was I had no idea how Jonah would react to me making an appointment for us to go to marriage counseling. Part of me felt like he had already checked out of marriage because that was the second time he threw divorce in my face as an option. I went to pick the kids up from Nikki and Kobe's house this morning after going to visit Leslie in the hospital. Luckily Leslie was in good spirits.

"Hey, Brii. How are you doing?" Trayce asked and I gave him a hug. He came into my house followed by Rolonda and their son Matthew.

"Hey, Matthew you are getting so big. Come give Auntie Brii a hug." I squealed. Matthew ran into my arms and I gave him a big hug.

"Where Nette and Blake at? Can I play with them?" Matthew gave me a little cheesy grin that lit up the entire room. He quickly squeezed out of my embrace and he was a spitting image of Trayce.

"May I go play with them? Yes, you can Matt. They are in the playroom." I grabbed his hand and led him to the playroom where Antoinette and Blake were playing quietly.

"I will keep an eye on the kids. Ro wanted to talk to you in private." Trayce gave me another hug and then went in the playroom to watch the kids. I walked into the kitchen to see Ro putting together a plate of snacks.

"Girl are you pregnant again? You can't stay the hell out of my kitchen." I complained jokingly.

"Bih don't wish pregnancy on my ass. I am just now really getting my figure back from having Matthew," Ro complained and I thought she was crazy. Ro still had that curvy hourglass figure that she had three years ago and Matthew only helped her flaunt her already voluptuous curves.

"Ro you know you look damn good. I am surprised he hasn't knocked your ass up again. Trayce ass is crazy enough to try to poke holes in the fucking condoms," I joked.

"Brii I am surprised it lasted this long too. Right after I gave birth to Matthew I made sure I got my ass on birth control because I was not going to be having babies for the man every year. Trayce insists that he wants a damn football team and I am not with the shits. I have been taking my birth control religiously and if I didn't know any better I would say I was pregnant but that isn't possible." Ro took a sip of juice.

" That shit is possible when I replaced your birth control pills with fucking sugar pills," Trayce remarked as he walked into the kitchen.

"Where in the hell are the kids? I thought you were watching them. Stop ear hustling," Ro complained and they started bickering back and forth like an old married couple. It made me sad because this was the kind of time Jonah and I should be on. Hell, we should be living our best lives and enjoy raising our small family together but we were more divided than ever and it came down to the fact that I didn't want to have any biological kids.

"The kids are taking a nap. I put Matthew in the same bed with Blake. I hope you don't mind Brii." Trayce waved his hand in my face to get my attention.

"Oh no, you are fine. Sorry, I was a bit distracted," I apologized.

"Brii I am sorry for forcing you to go to the club. Trayce got dead in my ass when I got home telling me I was wrong for interfering in your marriage. I meant well but I set everything in motion for things to happen the way that they did."

"Ro you don't even know the half of it and Jonah and I might be headed towards a divorce," I admitted. Trayce frowned and I knew he had something to get off of his chest.

"I knew Jonah wasn't going to be happy about you entertaining another nigga but he couldn't have gotten that mad at you?" Ro looked confused.

"No well, Jonah brought me home. We were arguing and it got heated. I instigated it by spitting in his damn face but then Jonah slapped the shit out of me. I was shocked because he had never put his hands on me before. I knew he felt bad after he hit me because I could see it all over his face but I was disgusted and couldn't talk to him then. What really pissed me off was he threw divorce in my face again and I am tired of it." It felt like a weight lifted off of my shoulder once I confessed the issues that were bothering me.

"I am not saying it is right sis but men can't take the shit they dish out. Ro told me the reason why she dragged your ass to the club and you should have let his ass calm down instead of spit in his face. Bottom line, I am going to need to step in and talk to him because putting his hands on you is unacceptable," Trayce replied.

"It is and I am starting to feel like our marriage is doomed to fail. I think most of our issues stem from the fact that I don't want to have any biological children. I feel like our family is complete with my siblings and Leslie but Jonah wants kids of his own. Honestly, it gets overwhelming with the three that we have even with Jonah here to help me. I don't want to become one of those women that loses themselves and becomes one of those Stepford wives."

"Is the problem that you don't want to have kids or you are scared of losing your identity? It is ok to not want to have children because not all women do but you need to reflect and be honest with yourself. Maybe it is good for you and Jonah to take some time apart so you can figure out what it is that you want," Ro suggested.

I sat and thought about it and realized my fear came from losing my identity and my dysfunctional childhood. It felt like a light bulb was going off in my head. I was having an Aha moment and I realized that I was the problem in my marriage. I never completely healed from the things I went through in my childhood. I was just as broken as AJ was and I was carrying past baggage into my marriage. I knew that I needed to get some help if I ever wanted to move forward with or without Jonah....

# JONAH

"Jonah are you sure there is nothing I can do to convince you to stay a little longer?" Joseline batted her doe-shaped eyes at me. I could not believe I slipped up and fucked this bitch last night although my memory was a little fuzzy. After the fight with Brii, I ended up calling Joseline up to meet for drinks. I didn't think anything of it when she offered to have drinks ready for me at her hotel room because I wasn't thinking clearly. When I arrived she had a glass of Henny waiting for me and I eagerly took the shot without thinking twice about it. Now I woke up in a strange hotel room naked and I couldn't remember whether we used protection last night or not.

"No, I need to get to the hospital and go see my son. You should know since they are letting Les get discharged today," I reminded the bird-brained bitch. I needed to find a way to force her to take a Plan B pill because I was not going to have kids with random women.

"I am sure they won't discharge him for another hour or two. Let me call and check with Dr. Donaldson who is watching over Les now." Joseline looked a little too eager to get me to stay and it was turning me off especially since I suspect that she drugged a nigga. No way I would have fucked that aquarium fish egg pussy sober because she was stinking from a mile away.

"No there is no need for that. I am going to get going and I need you to get a plan B pill—"

"Nigga no you just did not tell me to go get contraceptive for our lovemaking last night. You knew the consequences of fucking me raw and I told you to let me go get a condom but you said no let me feel you Joseline." This bitch started head rolling and snapping her fingers acting ghetto as hell.

"Bitch you know your ass drugged me because I don't even remember fucking your tuna fish smelling ass!" I yelled and yoked her ass up against the wall. Joseline started turning blue in the face and I was a couple of seconds away from killing her ass.

I finally let her ass go and she started coughing and looked scared. Once she regained her senses, she started crying fake crocodile tears. "Jonah I don't know why you are treating me like this. You wanted this as much as I did. Now your ass has selective memory about fucking me and I bet it won't be so selective if I call that fat bitch of yours and tell her I had your dick in every hole of my body—"

"Bitch disrespect, my wife, one more time and you won't live to see another fucking day. Leave Brii's name out of your mouth and recognize I will never be with you. You have two choices: Take a Plan B or get that demon sucked out of you if you choose to come at me about a pregnancy. By the way, I made sure to take some pictures and store them in the cloud so I can send them to the state about your inappropriate sexual behavior with your patients." I grabbed her and slammed her head against the bedpost. Joseline started bleeding from her head and was unconscious and then I panicked.

I didn't mean to hurt her. I just wanted to get my point across for her to leave my family alone. No matter how bad the state of my marriage was I wasn't going to allow her to come for my wife. I was frozen because I was unsure about whether to call for an ambulance or get the hell out of dodge. I knew it would look more suspicious if I tried dragging her body out of here so that wasn't an option. I decided to call Klayton since Luca had a lot going on. Klayton answered on the first ring.

"Yo, what's up?" Klayton answered.

I quickly ran down the entire situation and I was pissed off at myself for putting myself in that situation. "Listen I know I fucked up but I can't have this shit coming back on me in any way," I explained.

"Man I was about to handle a situation at the warehouse but I am going to my men watch over this Darnell nigga for me and I will be there in ten minutes with a couple of my boys. Close the door and do not answer for anyone. I will text you when I get there." Klayton hung up and I was grateful that he was coming through for me.

What happened today was a huge wake-up call for me and I vowed I was going to do better and be more understanding and compassionate towards Brii's feelings. The real dilemma was should I be honest and tell her or should I take this to the grave? What kind of nigga would admit that he might have been drugged and taken advantage of? I never should have put myself in a position where I would react off of emotion and risk losing the best thing that ever happened to me which was my family...

# 16

## KLAYTON

Thank God I dropped Treasure off at my house and got her settled before going to take Darnell's raggedy ass to the warehouse. I was just pulling up to the warehouse when I got the phone call from Jonah and he got himself in a bad situation. I dragged Darnell's ass inside the warehouse and told a couple on my crew to keep an eye on Darnell before taking off like a bat out of hell to get to the hotel that Jonah was staying at. Normally I would have tied Darnell's ass up myself and made sure he was secured but if I was going to keep Jonah's ass out of jail I was going to have to get to him as fast as I could.

I arrived at the hotel ten minutes later and shot Jonah a text. I placed a mask on my face and told one of the niggas I brought with me to go disable the video camera and get the tape while I handled shit in the hotel. I made sure my ass was strapped because today was her last day on earth. I learned the hard way you can't give these ring around the rosy looking whores a second chance because they will either plot on your ass or send the FEDS after your ass. I checked my phone and saw the text with the room number on it and I started jogging in the direction of the room. I made it and knocked on the door twice.

"Who is it?" Jonah's voice sounded muffled.

"Room service my nigga. Open up so we can get the fuck outta here." I wanted to put a bullet between this bitch eyes and bounce. I had my clean-up crew come separately and they were right behind me waiting for my text.

Jonah opened the door and I could tell he was worried. "Thank you for looking out, my nigga."

"No worries. None of us are perfect and I have fucked up more times than you can count in the past. Where is this stinky bitch? It smells like rotten sardines and tuna in this motherfucker," I complained. You seriously needed a gas mask to enter this bitch and it should have been illegal to have a pussy that smells like a two-week-old tuna fish sandwich.

"Man I lost it after she disrespected Brii and I threw her ass against the headboard," Jonah admitted.

I grabbed my gun and shot her ass three times in the stomach and five times in the head to be sure she was dead. I grabbed my knife out of my pocket and cut the bitch head off and blood spilled everywhere. Luckily I was wearing gloves so my fingerprints couldn't be traced to any of this shit. It might have been overkill but I wanted to be sure this bitch couldn't come back from the dead.

"My clean-up crew is coming to clean this shit up and I have someone getting the video from the lobby so we should be good. I hope you dusted any of your fingerprints because you will be a suspect," I looked at Jonah expectantly.

"Shit hold up." Jonah started wiping down surfaces and then we ran out of the room towards my car. My nigga was already there in the car waiting for us.

"I got the video and in case there was a backup video I erased everything from the last twenty-four hours," Ke'Andre explained.

"Good looking out. I'm hit you up with something extra for looking out. Where do you want me to drop you off because I assume you are in the doghouse with Brii?" I asked Jonah.

"Drop me by the hospital. Les is supposed to be getting released today and I need to make sure I am there for him. Thanks again for coming through." Jonah was grateful and gave me dap.

"No worries and I am not judging your situation because I have done some fucked up shit in the past. I never ever thought I would be in the position to ever give any relationship advice but you need to decide if you want to make things work with Brii and stick to it. You can't do fuck shit and run because you are mad Jonah. I want to see you win man."

"I feel you but I can't even come to Brii with this. I don't even know what I should tell her. Would she really believe me if I told her that I might have been drugged and raped? She is going to think it is just an excuse for cheating but I have never been the type of nigga to cheat." Jonah was in a really tough position and I really didn't have any good advice. Secrets usually find a way to come to light and when they do the situation usually ends up looking worse than what it was.

"If it counts I believe you. Some of these bitches are out here real scandalous. I know a hoe that set one of my friends up by using a turkey baster to get pregnant. She grabbed a used condom from the trash can and shot up her own club thinking he was going to fund her lifestyle and he got stuck with the baby momma from hell for the next eighteen to twenty-one years," KeAndre offered.

" I feel you but if I am Brii would I believe the shit I would be selling. This sounds like one of those secrets that need to go to the grave." Jonah was trying to convince himself to not tell Brii. I was torn in the middle because I could understand why he didn't want to tell her. However, secrets always had a way of finding themselves out there in the open. If she finds out any other way then it coming from Jonah directly then the entire situation could backfire on Jonah and he could lose Brii for good.

"Man secrets always end up coming to life Jonah. The bigger

question is can you handle the consequences if Brii finds out from a source other than you?" I asked and continued driving back towards the warehouse.

"How the hell would she find out? We just sent that bitch to meet her maker and there is no one that could place me being at the hotel last night." Jonah high fived KeAndre who was nodding his head.

" Man you will be surprised how women find out shit they are like little inspector gadgets. Hell, Brii might have tracked your phone and saw that you were at a hotel after that argument."

"Man she kicked me out of the house and I had to go sleep somewhere. She might suspect something but she will never know the truth." Jonah was trying to convince himself. I had a feeling he was going to have to lose Brii to really appreciate her.

"Keep telling yourself that if it helps you sleep at night Jonah. Take it from me that it is always worse when what is done in the dark comes to light..."

# LUCA

I knew from the second I met Gigi that I planned on hiring her in some capacity. The only issue I had in hiring her was whether I could keep my dick in my pants around her. I knew it was unfair to project my own issues on to her, but there was something about Ms. Reynolds that unsettled me. She gives me the butterflies in my stomach that I felt with AJ and that scares me. Part of me hoped that Gigi would turn down my employment offer but part of me was excited at the chance to get to know her better. Speaking of the devil itself, Gigi was calling my business line.

"Hello?" I answered hoping I didn't sound too eager.

"Mr. Glover? I hope I am not disturbing you. I just wanted to let you know that I accept your job offer. When can I start?" Gigi asked.

"That is wonderful. When are you available to start? The sooner the better." I cleared my throat and didn't even notice my receptionist Brianna has walked into my office unannounced.

" I can start tomorrow if you would like. I would like to get my office set up and start reading on some of the cases that will be coming up." Gigi replied. I was impressed and it sounded like

Gigi is a hard worker which is something that I desperately needed. Lately, I had been burying my problems in work which was effective until I went home and remembered I wasn't on good terms with my sister.

"You can start tomorrow or on Monday if you like. Just let me know which is more comfortable for you."

"I can come in tomorrow. What time do you need me at the office?" Gigi asked.

"Come in around nine am. I will have breakfast and coffee ready for you and I will have Brianna order carry out from Panera Bread. Does that sound good?" I asked.

"No offense Luca but I don't trust that receptionist of yours and she is unprofessional. I will bring my own breakfast in—"

"No I mean I will take care of it personally Gigi. I want your first day on the job to go smoothly and I plan to talk to her about her behavior," I reassured Gigi and then ended the phone call. I turned to address Brianna and didn't even say a word. I just stared straight at her because she knew she was wrong for coming into my office unannounced.

"Luca I just wanted—"

"My name is Mr. Glover to you and not Luca. Brianna, I don't know how we got to this place but you need to know that all we have is a professional relationship and that is all that we will ever have. If that is an issue let me know and I can find your replacement," I stated firmly. After that crazy psycho bitch Suzanne from *Coke Gurls Cali*, I wasn't playing with these crazy bitches sexually harassing me in the workplace especially in my own damn law firm.

"Why are you treating me like this Mr. Glover? We didn't start having problems until you interviewed that red-headed witch," Brianna pointed out. She was delusional and as much as I didn't want to fire her I could see that she was going to be a problem.

"I don't owe you any explanation about the decisions that I make for my law firm. Brianna, you need to stay in your place as an employee. Trust me this is the last warning you will get before I send your ass to the unemployment line. I have been peeping the fact that you are attracted to me for a while and I didn't want to embarrass you. I am putting it all on the table and making it known that I will not be with you in any romantic manner and if you can't accept that then I will accept your resignation. Do you understand?" I asked staring Brianna straight in the eye. Brianna isn't an ugly woman but her thirsty ways made her unattractive. She is half white and half black with silky long black hair and a Kim Kardashian booty that cannot be concealed by her work attire. She has natural sex appeal and I was sure she could get many men because she is beautiful but I have no interest in her.

Brianna turned red in the face and I knew I had read her ass dead to right. " Luca I mean Mr. Glover maybe you misunderstood me. I was only looking out for your best interests and—"

"I am a grown ass man. I don't need a little girl like yourself looking out for me," I snapped, and I was already over this conversation. I softened my tone and started speaking again. "Listen, I am not trying to be rude but I do not want to send any sort of mixed message because nothing will ever happen between us romantically. This is my livelihood that I built from the ground up and I refuse to let anyone ruin that. You are bordering on a very thin line and if you even breathe funny then I will fire your ass. Are we clear?"

"Yes, sir crystal clear." Brianna stood up sarcastically. One of the buttons on her white cuffed blouse was unbuttoned and her ample cleavage was spilling out. What she failed to realize is I am not a simple man that thinks with his dick. I have self-control and plenty of it. I quickly diverted my eyes away from her so she wouldn't get any idea that her thot approach was working in any kind of way. She quickly walked out of my office and I was finally left to my thoughts. I picked up one of my client's case files and it was a case involving an alleged murder. Brian Phillips was accused of first-degree murder and he claims he was in the wrong place at the wrong time but I wasn't even so sure he is innocent as he claims. However, it wasn't my job to take the moral high ground because it was my job to represent him to the best of my ability as a lawyer. I spent the rest of my afternoon brushing up on the Phillips case and getting ready to represent him in court...

# 17

# TREASURE

I could not go home to deal with my family after the close call with Darnell's snake ass. I was very lucky that God sent Klayton in my direction or I would have been violated again and I don't know if I would have had the strength to overcome that. I was emailing my professors to see if I could do my coursework from home before I was too paranoid to go to school on my own. Klayton was out handling business and he reassured me that Darnell would be taken care of but he should have been home by now. I sent him a text and he claimed he would be here soon because he had to deal with another emergency situation so I understood. The least I could do was be his peace in the situation and have a home-cooked meal waiting for him so I decided to try to find something to cook. I found some stuff to make chicken wings and boxed macaroni and cheese so that would have to do until we went grocery shopping.

Klayton didn't have time to pick Danielle up from Trayce's house so she was staying the night over there. I knew I needed to call and check in with my family but I didn't want them worrying about me. I felt like I was becoming a burden on Luca and I needed some space after our argument. I reluctantly called my mom and she answered.

"Treasure where are you at? You should have been home from school by now," my mom fussed. I knew it was only coming from a caring place but at times it felt like my entire family suffocated me and didn't give me the space that I needed.

"Mom I am ok and I will be home in a few days. I need some space—"

"Is this about that argument you had with Luca? Come home and we will have a family meeting and talk this out. We need you at home with us," my mom begged and I could hear her crying. I never wanted to make my mom cry especially knowing I thought my mom had died three years ago.

"Please don't cry, mom. I just need some time to think and there is more going on with me than the argument with Luca. I promise to check in with you and give Genesis a kiss for me and tell her mommy loves her." I hung up the phone without waiting for my mom to respond. At this point, I couldn't take listening to my mom cry. I knew it was selfish but I was in my feelings over everything that had happened in the last few days. I had no desire to be around Luca or my parents right now.

I felt a pair of strong arms wrap around my body and I knew it was Klayton. I felt my body relax against his and I didn't even hear him come in the house. I felt safe and protected around this man and he was my Superman. I was starting to fall in love with him and that scared the shit out of me.

"Hey, I didn't even hear you come in. I was about to cook up this food I found for dinner—"

Klayton picked me up bridal style and carried me to his master bedroom. Any other man I would have been questioning his intentions but I felt safe and secure with this giant teddy bear. "Sssh. I need you to relax Treasure. I am going to order us some pizza for dinner. The only thing I want you to worry about is making sure you are ok because that piece of shit almost trauma-tized you again."

I immediately start sobbing because it felt like the weight of the world was on my shoulder. "I can't it almost happened again. You saved me Klayton and I can't thank you enough—"

Klayton held me against his rock hard chest and let me cry until I got it all off of my chest. "I promise you I will kill behind your ass Treasure. I don't know what this powerful connection is between us but I will die for you with no questions asked. When I saw that fuck nigga about to violate you I lost my damn mind Treasure. I can't even imagine what the hell you are thinking especially with your past. You can stay here as long as you need to and if Luca has a problem with it he can come see me."

"What did I ever do to deserve you Klayton? I just can't deal with my family right now and—"

" You don't have to explain what doesn't need to be explained. You are safe here and you will be anytime I am around you. I was going to go back to the warehouse and deal with Darnell but you were more of my priority Treasure. I need to be around you and I need you like I need air to breathe baby doll. I can't explain these feelings I have for you and I don't want to overwhelm you but I love hard and will protect you with everything in me," Klayton explained, and I felt loved and cherished.

"Thank you for being my support system Klayton. I don't know if I want to tell my family what happened with Darnell because even though you rescued me it would devastate my entire family. If Luca finds out he is going to act even worse than he is now and I can't continue living in a bubble. I just need time to come to term and cope with what happened because I need to stay strong so they don't sense anything is wrong other than my argument with Luca. I emailed my professors to see if they will let me finish my coursework from home. I just can't think about going back to class and honestly, I might transfer after this semester. I don't think I can handle having to go to class and remember that he almost raped me on campus," I admitted.

Klayton looked angry and I knew it wasn't directed towards me. "Don't give that bastard or Blach the power over you Treasure. You are stronger than you know. If you need to take time off to get right then do that but don't transfer schools or make that piece of shit run you out of there. Listen, if I have to drop you off pick you up and sit in your classes with you I will do that so you feel safe. Don't let your past dictate your future."

"I know, but I just don't want to take ten steps backward. I have come so far in the last three years and—"

"You will continue making progress Treasure. I think you should make an appointment with your counselor and start seeing her once a week again if need be. You won't be good for anyone else until you are good for yourself—" Klayton was interrupted by his cell phone ringing and I could tell he didn't want to answer it. "Go ahead and answer that Klayton. I don't want to intrude on your personal business." I got up out of his embrace and laid down across his bed.

He started yelling into the phone and I knew it wasn't good news by the look he gave me after he hung up the phone. "Listen, I gotta go handle some shit but I will be back as soon as I find out more information. Apparently, that fuck nigga Darnell managed to escape from the warehouse and is on the run..."

# BRII

"Jonah, what do you want? I have no words for you right now nigga." I gave Jonah a blank stare. I was starting to emotionally check out of my marriage and I had no idea of what I wanted to do about my marriage. I needed a clear cut sign of whether my marriage could be saved or not. It would be unfortunate to take away the only stability that the kids have known but I also couldn't be unhappy. I felt like Jonah and I both changed and for the worst. It was like we were strangers in our own home.

"Brii I really want us to work things out. I picked Leslie up from the hospital and he is staying with me at the hotel but he deserves to be in his own home," Jonah started, but I interrupted him.

"Leslie can come to be in his own home. You aren't welcome here though," I stated nonchalantly and Leslie hobbled in the room.

"Mommy Brii may I please have some apple juice?" Leslie asked me tentatively. It almost appeared as if he scared me which was the last thing I wanted. I love him like he was my own blood-related child.

"Sure baby. Let me get it for you. Go back and play in the

playroom with Antoinette and Blake and I will bring you some snacks in a few minutes." I smiled at Leslie and he started to relax around me. I don't know why he felt so uncomfortable around me lately but I needed to find out what that was about.

"Mommy Brii do you hate me? If I been bad I'm sorry." Leslie had tears in his eyes like he was about to cry. I bent down to meet Leslie at eye level.

"I could never hate you, Leslie. Why do you think that?" I asked.

"You didn't come see me when I was in the hospital. I thought you didn't love me or daddy anymore." Leslie started crying and I was at a loss. Granted, I haven't been to the hospital since he was admitted but that was out of guilt. Deep down, I blamed myself for Leslie getting hit by a car and after getting into it with that doctor, I had no desire to go visit. Now I felt like shit because he noticed I haven't been there to visit him.

"Leslie I am sorry I didn't visit you. I was selfish and mean to not visit you but I don't hate you. I love you this much. I don't ever want you to feel like I don't care about you. Sometimes, adults make boo boos and I messed up by not visiting you. Will you forgive me?" I asked. I held my arms out very wide so he could see how much I love him.

"I forgive you. Leslie loves Mommy Brii." Leslie smiled. Children are so innocent and forgiving even when forgiveness isn't deserved.

"I am going to bring the snacks in. Go ahead and plan with Antoinette and Brii. If you want to come home and play with them you are more than welcome."

Leslie wheeled himself back to the playroom in the wheelchair the hospital gave him.

"You got some nerve trying to act like the mother of the year Brii when you didn't even visit Les when he was in the hospital. Then you want to take him from me and welcome him home yet I can't come home. What kind of bullshit is this? At the end of the day that is my child." Jonah's face was bright red and he was big fucking mad.

"Now Leslie is your kid nigga when you got a DNA test done proving you weren't the fucking father—"

Jonah quickly yoked my ass up against the wall. "I don't give a fuck if Les and I share blood or not but I have raised that the child the same way I have helped raise your siblings with no fucking complaints. You are not going to play my ass out here like I am a fucking simp ass nigga. I love you Brii but I am tired of the walls and barriers that you still put up with me. No matter what I do I can't get you to open up to me or trust me. In many ways, I feel like I am dealing with the same guarded Brii that I met back in the day." Jonah confessed and I was shocked to hear how he was really feeling.

We had more issues than I even knew that we had and I had no idea Jonah felt this way. We clearly needed some time and space to figure out if this marriage was what we wanted. "I had no idea you really felt that way." My voice cracked and I was heartbroken.

Jonah looked devastated and I could tell this was something he was just realizing. "Brii, we have been through so much together and our love is worth fighting for. Somewhere down the line, our marriage became toxic and I love you enough to let you go. If we are meant to be then we will find our way back to each other, but this isn't healthy for us or for the kids. Please don't cry Brii. I really don't want to hurt you."

Jonah gathered me in his arms as I sobbed. I could not believe this was how our love story was going to end. I love this man more than life itself and my woman's intuition was going off. Part of me felt like there was more to this than what he was saying but did I really want to know?

"Why didn't you tell me this was how you feel Jonah? How can you say our love is worth fighting for and then give me some swan song about letting me go?" I asked confused. Part of me knew that Jonah and I needed a separation but part of me still yearned to be with this man. I didn't understand it but the heart wants what the heart wants.

"I love you Brii but this isn't working out and this might be for the best. Let me go say goodbye to the kids." Jonah gave me a kiss on the cheek and walked out of the room leaving me in shock. I could not believe that Jonah was leaving me even though technically I kicked him out of our home. I always thought we would calm down and work it out like we always do.It was time for me to do some investigating of my own because Jonah was acting funny. Little did he know I had a secret of my own but now I knew I wasn't saying anything because I didn't want him staying with me out of pity. I found out I am three months pregnant but now I wasn't sure if I was keeping the unborn baby...

# 18

# HOPE

It was time to go back to New York and things were not in a good place with my family. I was unsure about leaving while things were rocky between Luca and Treasure and it was time for me to speak to Giovanni about it. Treasure still hadn't come home since our last conversation and Luca has been burying himself with work only coming home to sleep and leave early the next morning.

"Gio is Genesis down for a nap?" I asked him. He was in the kitchen pouring us both a cup of coffee.

"Yes, I just checked on her and she is doing fine. It is a damn shame because Treasure really hasn't spent much time with her since she has been home. I thought she was making progress moving on from the past, but I can't believe that she would put a man above her child." Giovanni shook his head. There has to be more to this than meets the eye because there is no way my child would disappear the way she did for no reason. I knew the argument with Luca had to do with it, but there was more to this and I needed to find out what was going on.

My woman's intuition was telling me that there was more to this situation than what we knew. She probably was at Klayton's house, but she probably felt like she couldn't come home since the argument with Luca. "I really don't think Treasure is putting Klayton above her own child. Something is going on with her. A mother knows Gio and something isn't right. She hasn't been answering the phone since the last time I talked to her and I can feel it that something is wrong with my youngest child."

"Listen, Hope, I love Genesis and Treasure with everything in me. I have been thinking about this and praying for a sign on this. I really think we should have Treasure sign her rights away. I have held out hope for years that she would come around and be ready to take custody of Genesis but—"

"Gio we don't even know the entire situation. That girl loves her daughter and the fact you would insinuate otherwise is pissing me off. I raised her my entire life and—"

"So that is what we are doing now Hope? Are we really throwing jabs because I wasn't around when Luca and Treasure were younger? I thought we were better than this Hope." Giovanni looked disappointed. That was an obvious sore spot for him because he felt bad about not being around to raise them when they were younger and I felt remorseful for what I said.

"I'm sorry Gio but you are making assumptions about our daughter without understanding the entire situation. Hell, neither of us knows what is going on right now so we need to sit back and wait until we find out what is going on with Treasure. I know her like the back of my hand and she wouldn't just pull a disappearing act if she didn't have a reason." I was going hard for my daughter because my intuition never lies to me.

"I am sorry for snapping on you Hope but this entire situation has me on edge. I just don't understand why she hasn't come home and won't answer our calls. Let me call that nigga Klayton. I got his number and maybe he will give me some answers," Giovanni suggested.

"Hell, it is worth a shot. We have nothing else to lose at this point." I shrugged my shoulders. Genesis only knows Treasure as her sister because we thought that was the best way to go until we knew if Treasure would step up and be a full-time mother.

Giovanni went to grab his phone and he called Klayton but only got his voicemail. "Dammit!" Gio roared. He threw his phone to the ground and the screen shattered into tiny little pieces.

"Gio calm down. We can't go back to New York with things being a mess right now. Our kids need us here," I whispered.

" I know Hope. Call me crazy and I don't know how you are going to feel about this because our lives are in New York but I was thinking we should move back to Los Angeles on a permanent basis. We can find Genesis a school out here and Treasure can see her more often and bond with her. If we move back here, that can help us make a more solid decision on whether we need to get permanent custody of Genesis." Giovanni explained.

"My life is wherever my children are and I think you might be on to a good idea. This could really work especially with Genesis being a candidate for eye surgery. When would we move back?" I asked.

"Considering we told Dr. Schulman that we are all in on the surgery you can stay here with Genesis and get her ready for surgery. I can go back to New York and tie up any loose ends and get back in time for the surgery."

"Will, that really work? What if something goes wrong?" I asked. It sounded like a good plan but all sorts of things could go wrong.

"There isn't a plan out there that is foolproof but if anything happens with you Genesis Luca or Treasure my ass will be on the first red-eye back to be near you guys. You have my word I am not going to abandon you guys. My family is my world and having a second chance with you guys means everything to me," Giovanni explained and I started to relax.

Giovanni's word is bond and I knew this man like the back of my hand. When he broke up with me many years ago, he did that for my own good. Everything he does is meant to make his family better. "Ok, babe so what can I do to make this easier on you? I want to be your helpmate and your companion. If you are stressed then I am stressed too. We need to call a family meeting but how in the hell can we get Luca and Treasure in the same place?" I started biting my nails which was a bad habit of mine.

"I will take care of Luca if you take care of Treasure. I know you haven't been able to really talk to her but I am going to give you Klayton's number so you can continue reaching out to him…"

# GIGI

It was my first day on the job and Luca insisted on me on me calling him Luca instead of Mr. Glover.

"Are you sure you are good? I want you to be comfortable. Feel free to decorate your office the way you would like. I went to Panera and picked up breakfast for everyone in the office. I have a few folders with some cases so you can start reading and getting familiar with the cases. Do you have any questions?" Luca asked.

"No, thank you. I am good." I smiled. I grabbed some coffee and croissants and brought my meal back to my desk. I saw that bitch Brianna trying to cheese in Luca's face and he wasn't even stunting her ass. I don't know why I was jealous but I didn't like it. There was no room in my life for love because I am focused on my career. Love doesn't pay the bills or keep a bih warm at night so there was no room for it in the Reynolds household.

I ate my breakfast and then started to get to work decorating my area with Christmas decorations. Shit, Halloween was next week but I always loved the holidays and wanted to make my work area inviting for myself and clients.

"Excuse me. I just wanted to tell you that Luca is mine and

you better keep your paws off of him. I have been putting in work to get close to Luca and he might not know it but I am his future wife." Brianna stepped into my personal space.

"First of all, get out of my personal space. I do not want Luca nor am I threatened by your petty little threats. I will sue your ass for harassment if you don't leave me alone. I know how to use the law to my advantage and every time you try me I will be documenting and recording," I snapped.

" California law dictates you can't record without having the other person's consent so good luck using that shit in court bitch." Brianna pushed me and I tripped over my chair and fell to the ground. I felt humiliated because this little heifer pushed me around in the workplace. She had a smirk on her face because she knew I didn't want to risk my job, especially on the first fucking day. That was the only thing saving her at this point.

"Brianna please go to my office. What are you doing at Gigi's desk? It looks like she was minding her business and you hit her—"

"Luca she got in my face and told me to come to her office so she could fight me. Gigi said she wanted to beat my ass because she has a crush on you. I was here before she and I will be here after her and you need to check this witch—"

"BRIANNA TO MY OFFICE NOW!" Luca's voice roared and I was shaking at the way he yelled at her.

She quickly ran to do what she was told. Luca walked over to help me up. "Are you ok Gigi?"

"Yes, I am fine. Listen I know this is my first day but I don't think this will work with both of us in the office. I will end up catching an assault charge and losing my license."

Luca started laughing and there was something innately sexy about his laugh. It turned me on in the worst way and my panties were drenched. " I am sorry for her behavior. I saw her push you and I know damn well you didn't start that altercation. Trust me when I say that the situation will be handled." Luca reassured me.

"Get her in check Luca because she can be a problem for your law firm. She looks like one of those petty spiteful bitches so make sure you are documenting everything," I warned Luca and he walked back into his office to handle Brianna.

The rest of my day went uneventfully and I finally made it home around six pm. I saw a strange Lincoln Navigator parked outside of my apartment complex but paid it no mind because I figured it was for one of the other tenants. I got out and made sure my car was locked before I headed towards my apartment. I walked up the stairs with my briefcase in hand and was digging in my purse for the keys to my apartment. I grabbed my keys and was about to try to open my door when I saw my worst nightmare standing by my front door and it was my ex-boyfriend James.

"What the fuck are you doing here?" I asked.

"Regina is that how you greet an old friend? I thought you would be happy to see me. After all, you only tried ruining my career but I am here to show you that karma is a bitch and you will be getting yours soon." James had a sinister smile on his face. Why the fuck did he decide to pop up on me now and how the hell did he find me?

"Fuck you, James. You needed to get exposed for the dirty dick booty bandit bastard that you are. You could have given me all sorts of diseases with your down low ass." I spit in his face and then I reached in my purse to grab my mace.

"You fucking bitch!" James tried to slap me but I kicked him in the groin and then maced his ass one good time. He was on the ground in extreme pain. I took the chance to run for it which was extremely difficult in high heels. I was cussing myself out for trying to look cute on the first day of the job and I should have worn a pair of flats.

Luckily James was in enough pain where he couldn't follow

after me and I made it back to my car. I got in my car and sped out of my apartment complex like a bat out of hell. I needed to lay low and get a hotel room so I could figure out what my next move would be...

# 19

# KLAYTON

When I held Treasure in my arms and she cried it did something to me that even Shae was never able to do. I thought I was in love with my ex but that was definitely puppy love compared to how I was feeling about Treasure. I hurt with Treasure like I was the one that was being violated and that nigga Darnell was going to feel me. Meanwhile, I was at the warehouse and I called my nigga Trayce to come to help me give a dose of punishment. I toyed with the idea of calling Luca but we weren't on good terms and he had no idea what had happened recently. It wasn't my place to say anything. If Treasure wanted him to know about Darnell almost raping her then it would be up to her to tell him because I am not a snitch.

"Yo what the fuck were you niggas doing when I left you guys here to watch Darnell? I had an emergency that I had to handle and I had you guys on straight orders to not let Darnell go." My trigger finger was itching and I felt Trayce's hand on my shoulder.

"Calm down bruh. Let's hear what these fuck boys got to say for fucking around on your dime." Trayce had really chilled out since he retired from the streets. He used to believe in the motto shoot first and ask questions later but he had really mellowed out since he married Rolonda.

"Listen Klayton we fucked up but let us make it right. I told this nigga here not to sneak no girls in the warehouse and pussy would be his downfall." This little jack boy named Ronald started singing like a fish. So, these niggas ended up losing Darnell because they got caught up in pussy?

"Was the pussy good? Did that snatch steal your soul? I hope that was some grade A pussy you guys got because this is not going to end well for you." I was pacing back and forth with a Glock in my hand.

"Man I fucked up. You know how it is when these broads give you some grade A sloppy toppy. We got caught slipping. Just give us the chance to make things right." Blue one of my other workers started pleading for his life. He should have thought about that when he was fucking on the job.

"Do I not pay you, niggas, well? I always look after my team and I expect that loyalty to be given in return. When your son needed chemotherapy for his cancer treatments I paid for all of them and covered your expenses while you were unable to work for me Blue. I made sure your entire family was good. And you Ronald I pay for your grandmother's funeral when she died from Alzheimer's and covered her expenses for the nursing home she was in without even docking your pay. This is what the hell I get in return. That nigga you let get away not only stole drugs and got high off of my supply taking money from all of our mouths, but he almost raped someone near and dear to me. That alone is a violation worthy of death and do you know what I do to the idiots that let him get away?" This vent session was doing me some good. Normally I would shoot their ass and be done with it, but I needed to let some of my frustrations loose. Before I called them to the warehouse, I drove by campus to see if Darnell was dumb enough to go back knowing I was going to be looking for his ass but he wasn't there. Luckily I had a plan that involved his elderly parents and I would draw him out using them.

"Klayton let us make things right. You have always been good to us and this was a lapse of judgment on our part," Ronald admitted.

I untied Ronald and he looked relieved until I grabbed him and dragged him in front of Jackson. "Here is my Glock. You have a choice to make. Either you kill him or you kill yourself. Who will it be?"

Trayce was looking at me like I lost my mind. He had his gun out pointed at Ronald so he knew not to try any funny shit.

"Klayton Jackson is my best friend and—"

"You have until the count of ten to make a decision and you better hope you make the right one or Trayce will make it for you," I replied and then started counting. I had made it down to the number two when a gun went off.

**Pow! Pow! Tata! Tata!**

The gunfire ceased and I saw both Ronald and Jackson's dead bodies lying there in a pool of blood. "Good work big bro. I almost thought you got soft and lost your touch man." I joked. Trayce and I went to work disposing of their bodies ourselves so we could be sure this wouldn't come back to bite us.

"Yo, you got soft Klayton. You in here kee keeing with niggas having entire conversations when you used to blow people's heads off," Trayce clowned.

"Man I am trying to take a more sane approach nigga—" I was interrupted by my phone ringing and I saw it was Hope calling. I gestured for Trayce to hold on so I could take the phone call.

"Mrs. Glover? Is everything ok?" I asked calmly. I figured she was calling because Treasure has been staying at my house. I just needed to be sure nothing else had popped off.

"Hi Klayton. I was hoping you would let me speak to Treasure. She hasn't been returning my calls since the last time I talked to her and I am worried about her." Hope admitted and I felt bad but at the end of the day, my loyalty ultimately rides with Treasure.

"Listen Mrs. Glover all I can tell is you is Treasure is safe with me at my house. When she is ready to come home I will bring her home. She is going through some issues that she isn't comfortable opening up to you guys about but when she is ready she will talk to you. I am big on family so I wouldn't let too much time go before she comes back home especially knowing that she has a daughter."

"Can I at least speak with her? I just want to hear her voice and be sure that she is ok. You have a daughter Klayton. What would you do if you were in my shoes?" Hope asked and I felt guilty. I was torn between a rock and a hard place.

"I feel for you but I am not home with Treasure at the moment. I had to handle some business but I will tell her to call you." Hell, it was the least I could do to try to give my future mother-in-law some comfort.

"Klayton, I just need one favor. Please try to bring her home on Monday evening for a family meeting. It is important that we get Treasure and Luca in the same room so they can hash out their differences and I can try to get Treasure to open up on what is going on with her. I know there is more to this than her argument with her brother." Hope explained.

"What time is the meeting Monday? I promise to make sure Treasure is there even if I have to throw her in the trunk and drag her there..."

# TREASURE

I had ordered some take out for Klayton and me from Uber Eats and this Popeyes I ordered had hit the damn spot. I made Klayton a plate and put it in the microwave and waited for him to come home. When he did come home, I eagerly jumped into his arms and this felt natural like I was supposed to be here. I jumped into his arms and before I knew it I had kissed him on the lips catching us both off guard. His tongue slipped in my mouth and it felt like I was done for by the way he was kissing me back. I reluctantly ended the kiss and there was a sparkle in Klayton's eyes that wasn't there before.

"I am happy to see you too baby girl. What was that kiss for?" Klayton smiled at me and it made my day. Getting a smile out of Klayton made me forget about all of the drama that was in my life. It made me forget about all of the rainy days and made me think about all of the sunshine that he brought into my life.

"It is for being you. Did you eat while you were out? I ordered some Popeyes and put a plate in the microwave. I hope you like Popeyes. I put some chicken and macaroni and cheese and mashed potatoes on a plate for you," I rambled and I felt nervous for some reason. This man came back into my life and shook my world up and I didn't regret it for one second. Luca would eventually come around because I know my brother was only acting this way out of fear.

"That sounds delicious babe. Way better than KFC that white people chicken and shit. Popeyes from the hood so you know they are using seasoning on their damn chicken before they fry it. Why do I sense that I make you nervous?" Klayton asked.

"You are my Superman, Klayton. I love being around you and I feel this connection with you right here." I pointed to my heart. I walked into the kitchen and grabbed his plate of food and brought it to him with a cold beer from his refrigerator. Klayton sat down and started tearing his food up.

Klayton stopped eating and stared directly at me. "It is good to know what I am feeling for you is reciprocated Treasure. I didn't want to say anything while all of this is going on and you feel overwhelmed. You already have more drama than a little bit to deal with. I want to bring you peace love and prosperity and not pain." Klayton admitted. Was that love I saw in his eyes for me? I never thought I would see the day that a man fell in love with me and wasn't trying to use me for my body.

"You are the best thing besides my daughter that I have in my life Klayton. You have been my hero and my Superman and I am falling for you. I never ever wanted to fall in love after Blach damaged me but you forced your way into my heart Klayton." Tears were sliding down my face as I poured my heart out to Klayton.

"Treasure are you sure? I don't want you to feel pressured into saying something that you aren't sure of. I want to be with you and I want to take things slowly until you are ready." Klayton has a big heart but I wish he would take me seriously with me pouring my heart out.

"Klayton don't play with how I feel. That is one of the biggest issues I have with my family. They never take what I am feeling seriously!" I screamed and I could feel myself getting upset.

Everyone treated me like a fragile piece of glass that would break if not handled carefully.

"Treasure I am not trying to play you or make you feel like I am not taking you seriously. I just don't want you to feel like you have to say something because I care about you. I am falling in love with you and I don't want to force you into anything." Klayton walked over and held my hand.

"You really love me Klayton? Are you sure?" It was almost too good to be true that a man like Klayton would fall in love with a girl like me. It felt like I was living in a dream and I hadn't woken up yet.

"Baby girl I know that I have never felt the way I feel for you with any other woman including my ex-girlfriend Shae. I know you are not ready for a serious relationship yet but—"

"How can you tell me what I am ready for or not Klayton? Stop trying to speak for me just like Luca tries to do. I have my own voice and I want to be heard Klayton. I know what I feel and I am falling in love. It is cool that you don't care for me the way you claim you do, but don't lie to me just to make me feel better. Klayton I better go back home. This has been good while it has lasted." I got up and went into the bedroom to grab my purse before I could grab my purse Klayton picked me up and carried me to his bedroom. I was kicking and screaming for him to put me down but he wouldn't listen.

"Don't put any words in my mouth. I want to take my time and build a solid foundation with you. I am not Blach or Darnell. Those fuck niggas just wanted to take advantage of you and—"

**Boom! Boom!**

Klayton and I both sat up as a loud explosion shattered our ears. Klayton and I got up and went to the window and saw the wired gate crumble to the ground. The crazy part was we didn't see any enemies coming for us so we had no idea where they were at. Suddenly the sound of gunshots started ringing out from inside of the house and I was terrified. Someone had gotten in but how? I clung to Klayton's leg and he shook me off and wrapped his strong arms around me.

"Klayton I am scared!" I whimpered and pee started dripping down my leg.

"Treasure I need you to boss up right now and trust a nigga. You say you love me right?" Klayton held my face close to his tenderly.

"Yes, I do bae. How are we going to get out of here?" I asked.

"We aren't going to get out of here. You are going to leave through the emergency passage I have built in the wall in the hallway. Follow me." Klayton started leading me to the secret tunnel.

"Why aren't you coming with me? What if they hurt you?"

"Baby girl I am Klayton Jackson and my black ass is not going down without a fight. I need you to listen and not fight me on this because time is of the essence. There is a set of keys on a rack in the tunnel they are keys to my BMW and the tunnel takes you straight to my car. Get it in and go straight home. Do you hear me?" Klayton instructed.

"Yes please be safe. I didn't fall in love with you just to lose you," I whimpered and Klayton gave me a passionate kiss that would stay in my memory forever. I prayed it wasn't the last kiss that I would ever get from the man I was in love with.

"Do not worry about me Treasure. I gotta go and figure out who is coming for me but I love you," Klayton pressed the code in a keypad and a secret tunnel opened. It was dark as hell but I made my way inside as the door closed on me. I saw the holder with a set of car keys on them and grabbed them and followed the path towards Klayton's car. My adrenaline was pumping and blood was rushing in my veins. I was scared yet excited to see what awaited me on this journey. I kept walking at a brisk pace until I saw a shiny black BMW come up in the distance and I smiled. I was about to get the hell out of dodge and prayed I heard from Klayton soon. He was equipped to deal with this kind of shit and I wasn't. I got closer and pressed the car alarm to unlock the door but things suddenly went terribly wrong. A loud explosion sounded that made my ears hurt.

**Boom!**

The last thought that I had was please let my baby girl Genesis be ok in death and for my parents to look after her before everything went all black and my soul started to leave my body...

**To be continued...**